TEEN TITANS GO!™

PRANK'D! AND DON'T LOOK

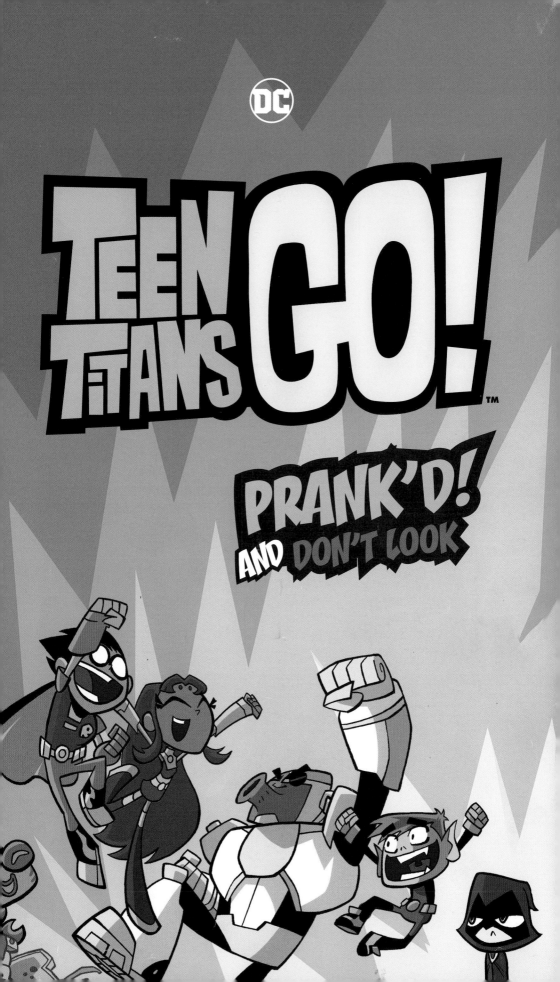

Teen Titans Go! is published by
Stone Arch Books,
A Capstone Imprint
1710 Roe Crest Drive
North Mankato, MN 56003
www.mycapstonepub.com

Library of Congress Cataloging-in-Publication Data is available at the Library of Congress website:
ISBN: 978-1-4965-7997-3 (library binding)
ISBN: 978-1-4965-8003-0 (eBook PDF)

Summary: How do the Teen Titans kill time in between missions? By making prank calls, of course! But what happens when
Beast Boy prank calls . . . Batman?! Then when a mysterious package arrives for Raven, the rest of the Titans work themselves
into a frenzy wondering, "What's in the box?!"

Alex Antone Editor – Original Series Paul Santos Editor

STONE ARCH BOOKS
Chris Harbo Editor
Brann Garvey Designer
Hilary Wacholz Art Director
Kathy McColley Production Specialist

Printed and bound in the USA
1965

TEEN TITANS GO!™

SHOLLY FISCH AMY WOLFRAM
WRITERS

JORGE CORONA LEA HERNANDEZ
ARTISTS

JEREMY LAWSON
COLORIST

WES ABBOTT
LETTERER

DAN HIPP
COVER ARTIST

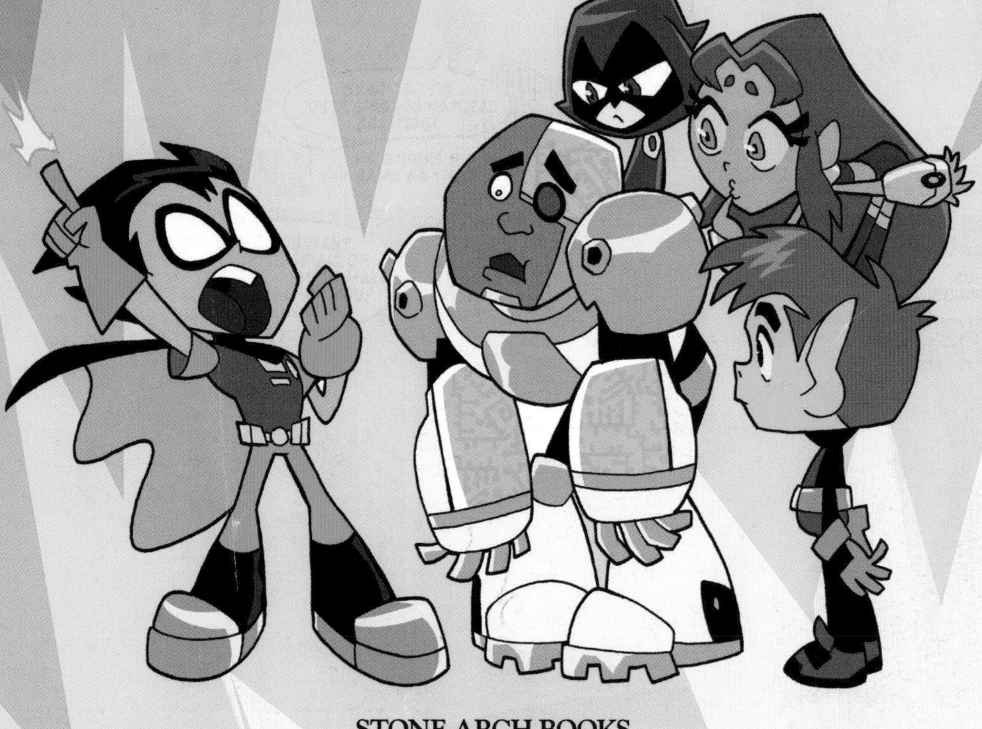

STONE ARCH BOOKS
a capstone imprint

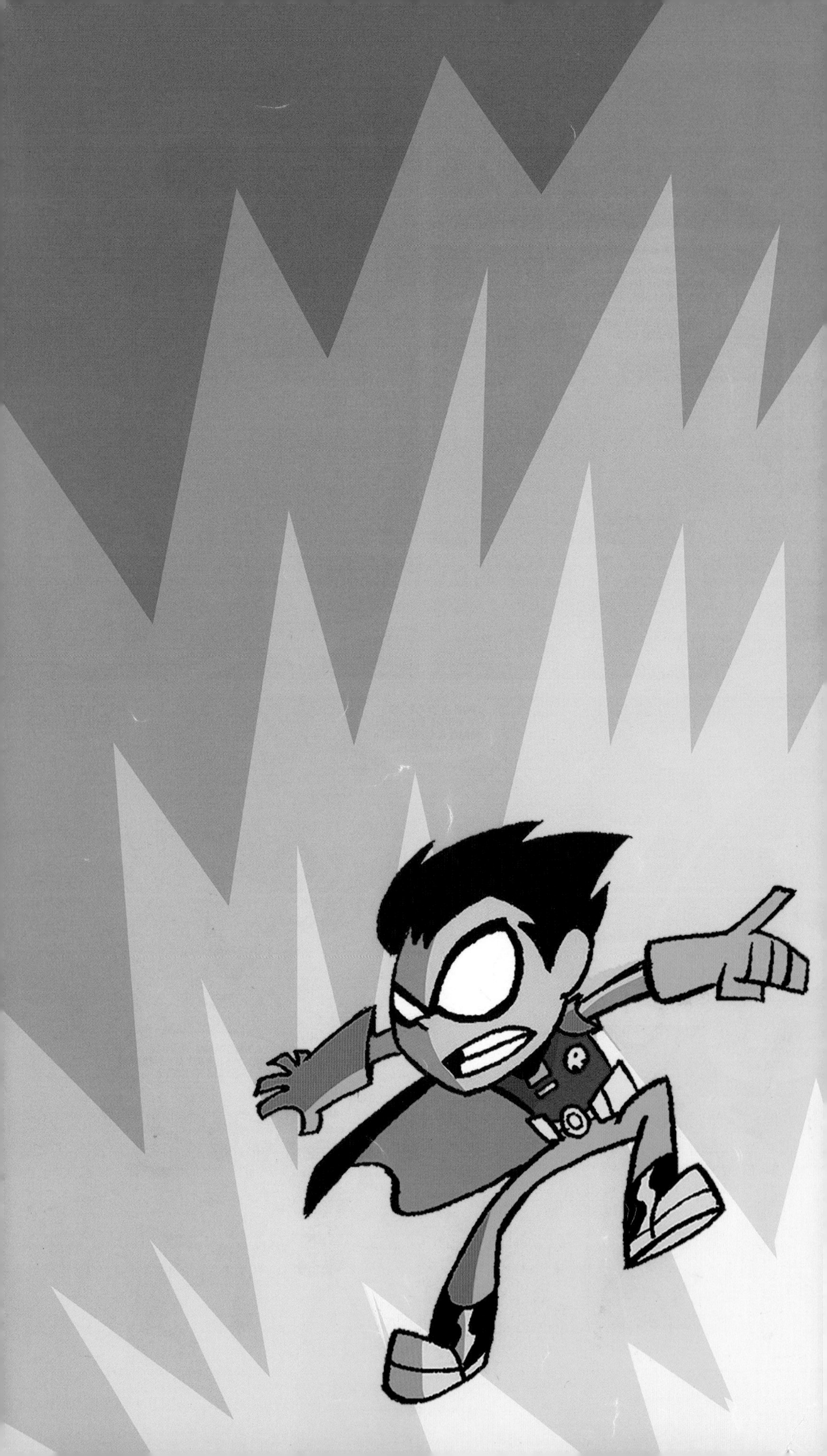

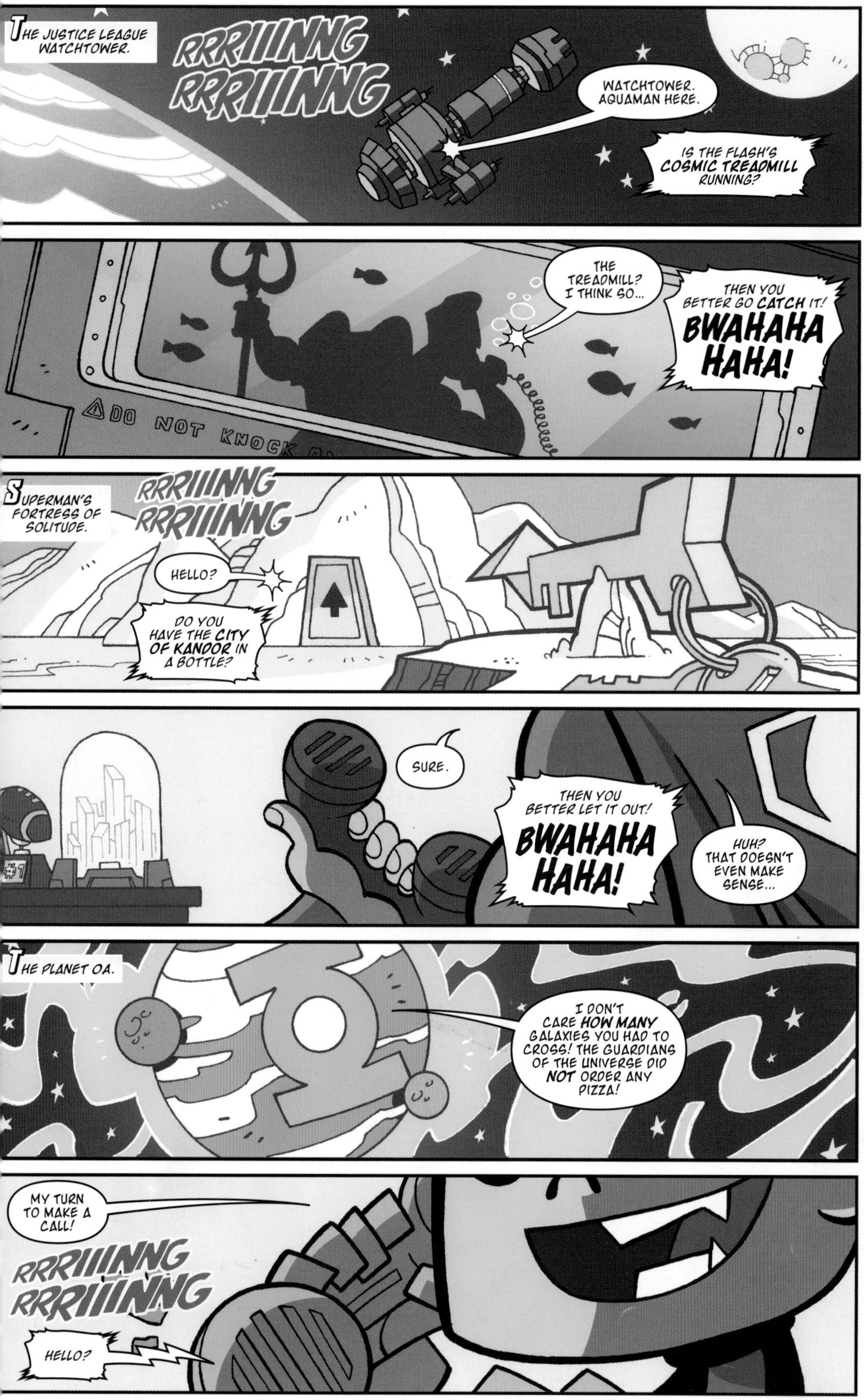
THE JUSTICE LEAGUE WATCHTOWER.
RRRIIINNG RRRIIINNG
WATCHTOWER. AQUAMAN HERE.
IS THE FLASH'S COSMIC TREADMILL RUNNING?
THE TREADMILL? I THINK SO...
THEN YOU BETTER GO CATCH IT! BWAHAHA HAHA!
DO NOT KNOCK
SUPERMAN'S FORTRESS OF SOLITUDE.
RRRIIINNG RRRIIINNG
HELLO?
DO YOU HAVE THE CITY OF KANDOR IN A BOTTLE?
SURE.
THEN YOU BETTER LET IT OUT! BWAHAHA HAHA!
HUH? THAT DOESN'T EVEN MAKE SENSE...
THE PLANET OA.
I DON'T CARE HOW MANY GALAXIES YOU HAD TO CROSS! THE GUARDIANS OF THE UNIVERSE DID NOT ORDER ANY PIZZA!
MY TURN TO MAKE A CALL!
RRRIIINNG RRRIIINNG
HELLO?

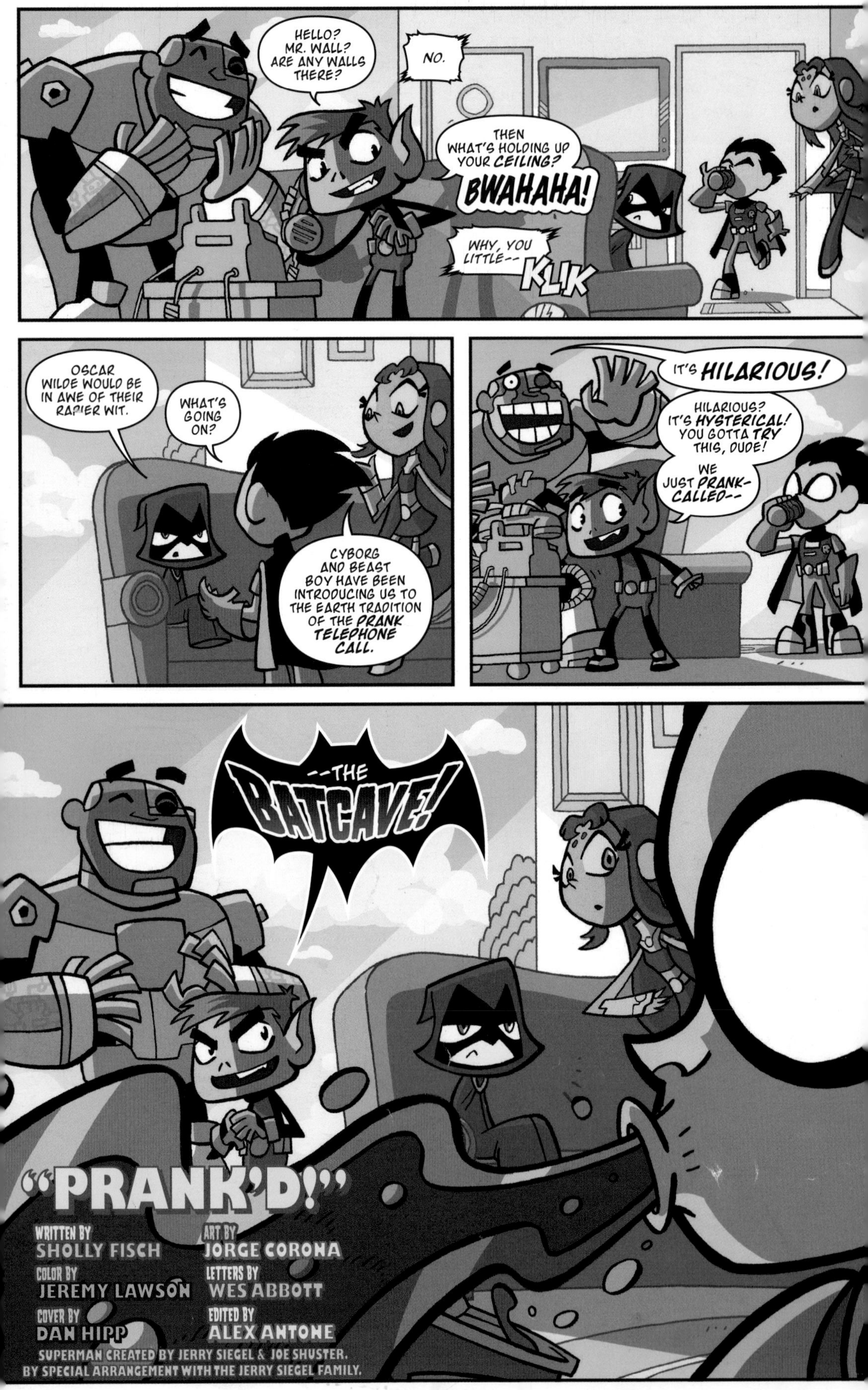

HELLO? MR. WALL? ARE ANY WALLS THERE?
NO.
THEN WHAT'S HOLDING UP YOUR CEILING?
BWAHAHA!
WHY, YOU LITTLE--
KLIK
OSCAR WILDE WOULD BE IN AWE OF THEIR RAPIER WIT.
WHAT'S GOING ON?
CYBORG AND BEAST BOY HAVE BEEN INTRODUCING US TO THE EARTH TRADITION OF THE PRANK TELEPHONE CALL.
IT'S HILARIOUS!
HILARIOUS? IT'S HYSTERICAL! YOU GOTTA TRY THIS, DUDE!
WE JUST PRANK-CALLED--
--THE BATCAVE!
"PRANK'D!"
WRITTEN BY SHOLLY FISCH
ART BY JORGE CORONA
COLOR BY JEREMY LAWSON
LETTERS BY WES ABBOTT
COVER BY DAN HIPP
EDITED BY ALEX ANTONE
SUPERMAN CREATED BY JERRY SIEGEL & JOE SHUSTER.
BY SPECIAL ARRANGEMENT WITH THE JERRY SIEGEL FAMILY.

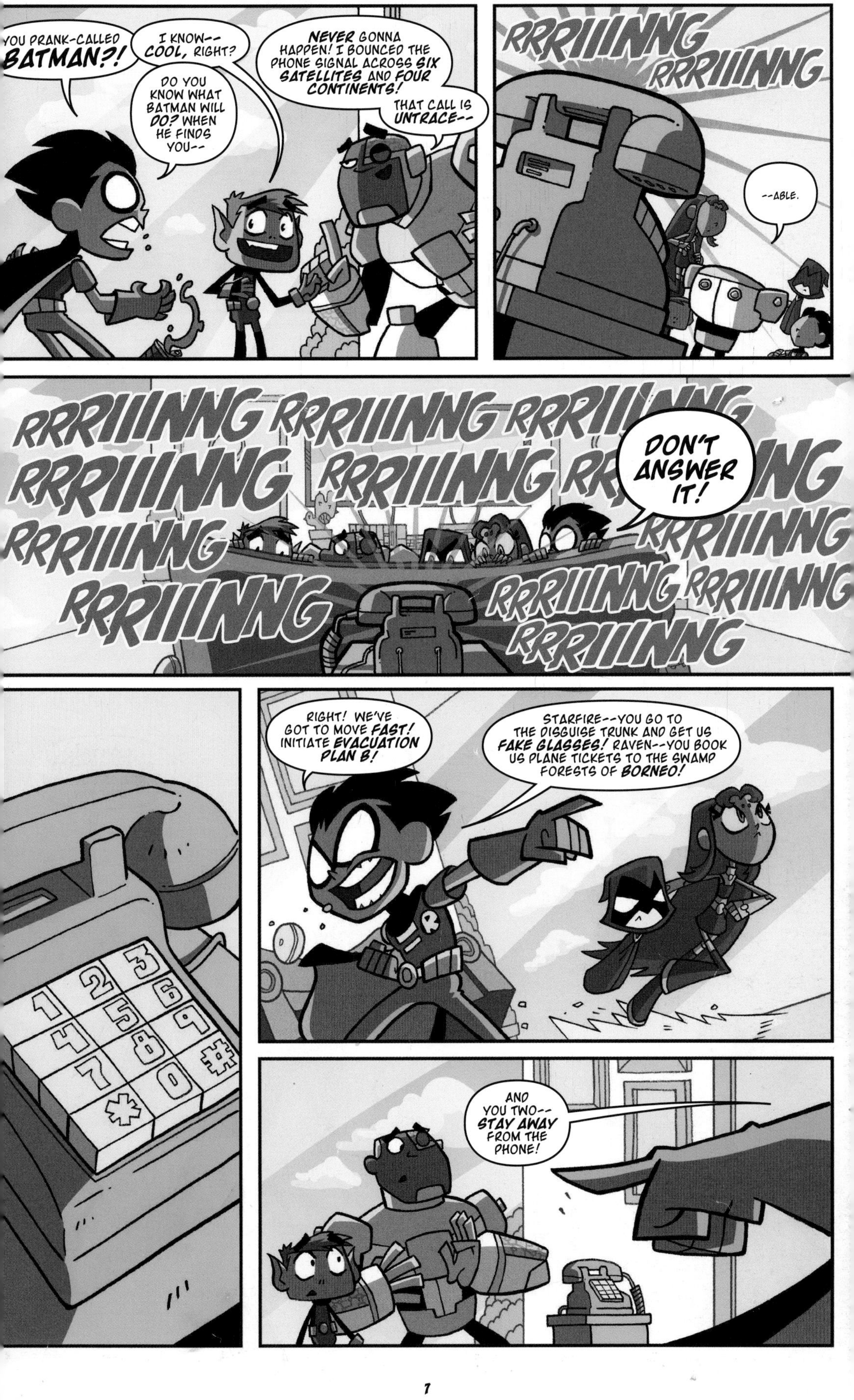
YOU PRANK-CALLED BATMAN?!
I KNOW--COOL, RIGHT?
DO YOU KNOW WHAT BATMAN WILL DO? WHEN HE FINDS YOU--
NEVER GONNA HAPPEN! I BOUNCED THE PHONE SIGNAL ACROSS SIX SATELLITES AND FOUR CONTINENTS!
THAT CALL IS UNTRACE--
RRRIIINNG RRRIIINNG
--ABLE.
RRRIIINNG RRRIIINNG RRRIIINNG
RRRIIINNG RRRIIINNG
DON'T ANSWER IT!
RRRIIINNG
RRRIIINNG
RRRIIINNG
RRRIIINNG RRRIIINNG
RRRIIINNG
1 2 3 4 5 6 7 8 9 * 0 #
RIGHT! WE'VE GOT TO MOVE FAST! INITIATE EVACUATION PLAN B!
STARFIRE--YOU GO TO THE DISGUISE TRUNK AND GET US FAKE GLASSES! RAVEN--YOU BOOK US PLANE TICKETS TO THE SWAMP FORESTS OF BORNEO!
AND YOU TWO--STAY AWAY FROM THE PHONE!

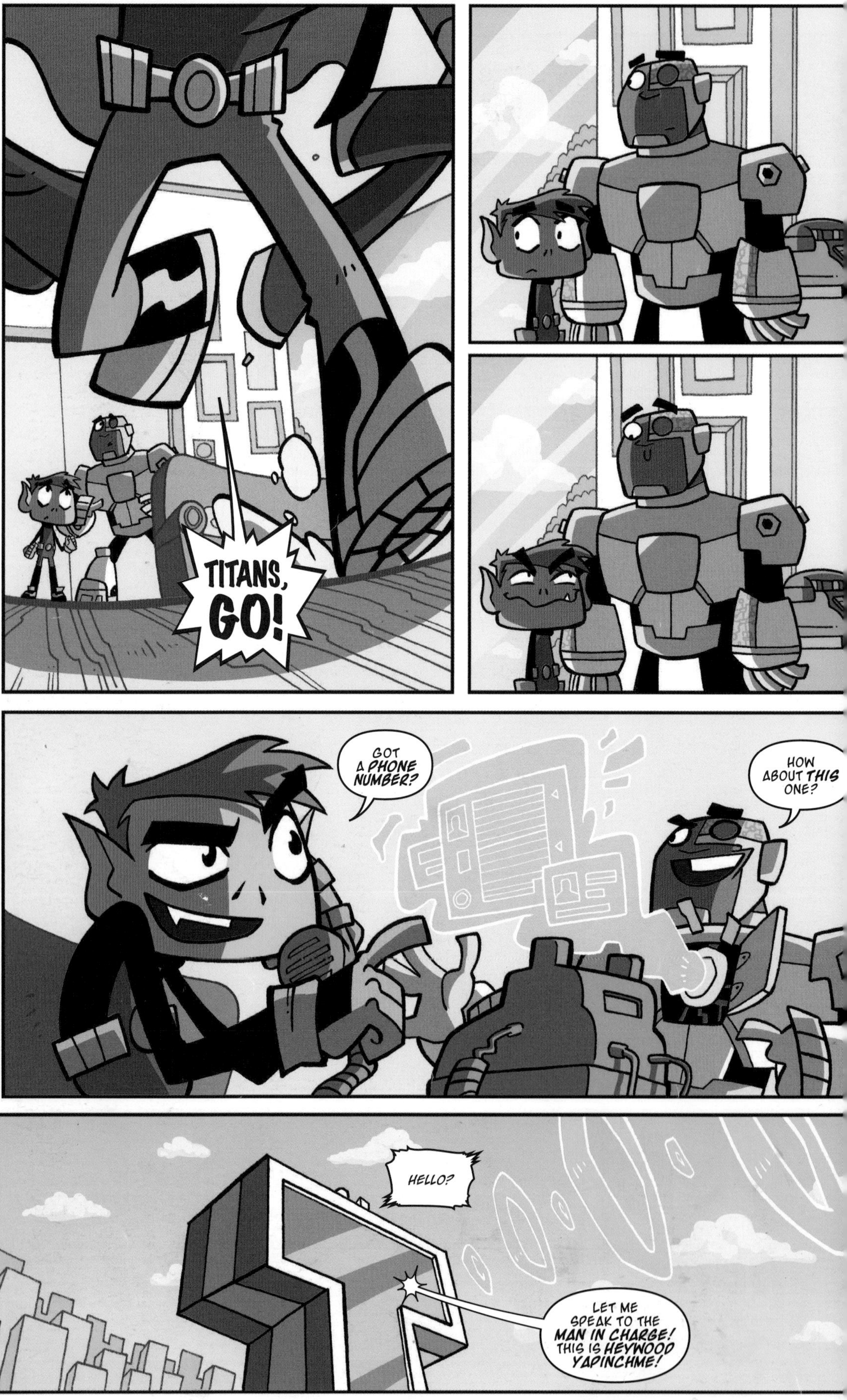
TITANS, GO!
GOT A PHONE NUMBER?
HOW ABOUT THIS ONE?
HELLO?
LET ME SPEAK TO THE MAN IN CHARGE! THIS IS HEYWOOD YAPINCHME!

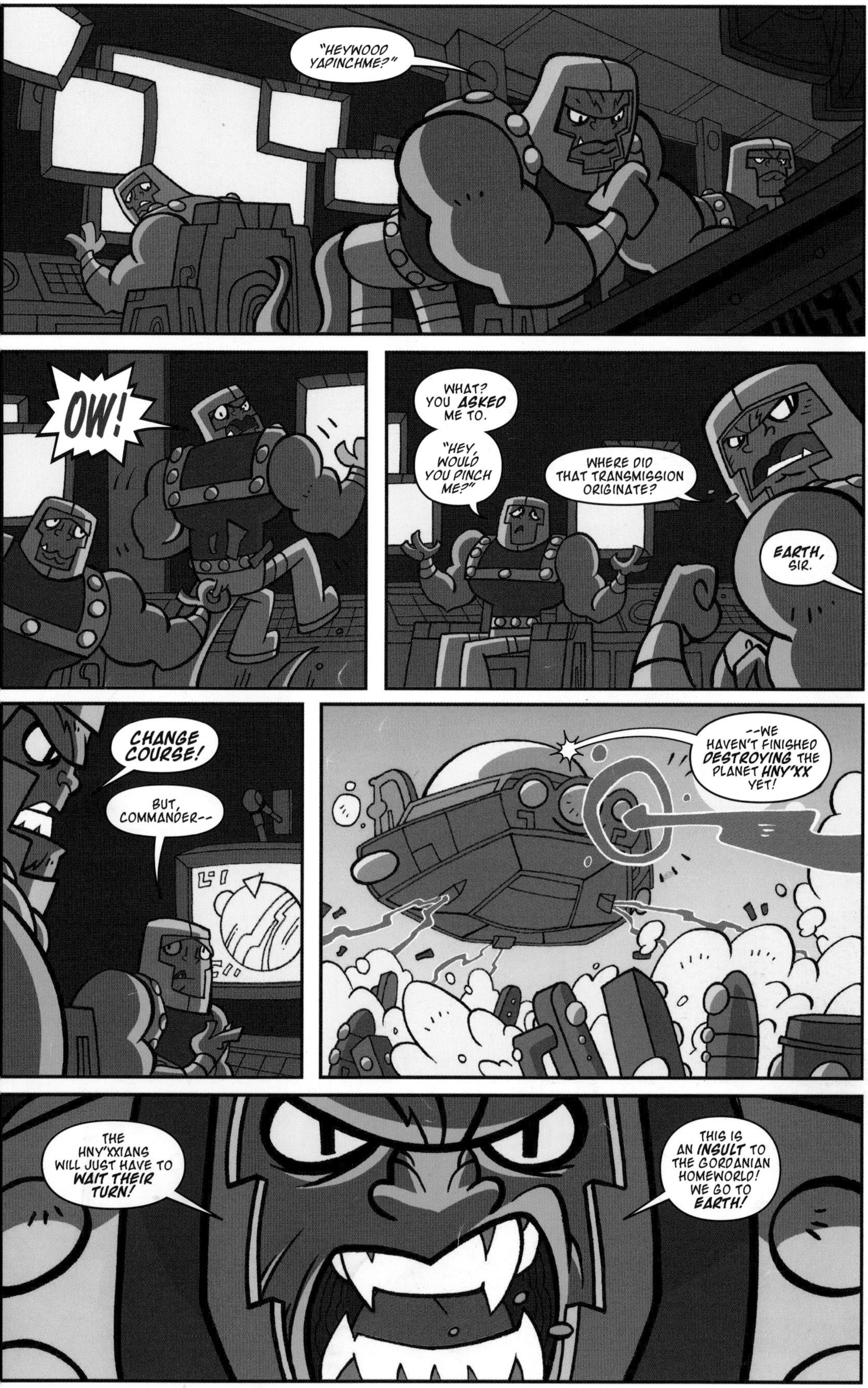

"HEYWOOD YAPINCHME?"
OW!
WHAT? YOU ASKED ME TO.
"HEY, WOULD YOU PINCH ME?"
WHERE DID THAT TRANSMISSION ORIGINATE?
EARTH, SIR.
CHANGE COURSE!
BUT, COMMANDER--
--WE HAVEN'T FINISHED DESTROYING THE PLANET HNY'XX YET!
THE HNY'XXIANS WILL JUST HAVE TO WAIT THEIR TURN!
THIS IS AN INSULT TO THE GORDANIAN HOMEWORLD! WE GO TO EARTH!

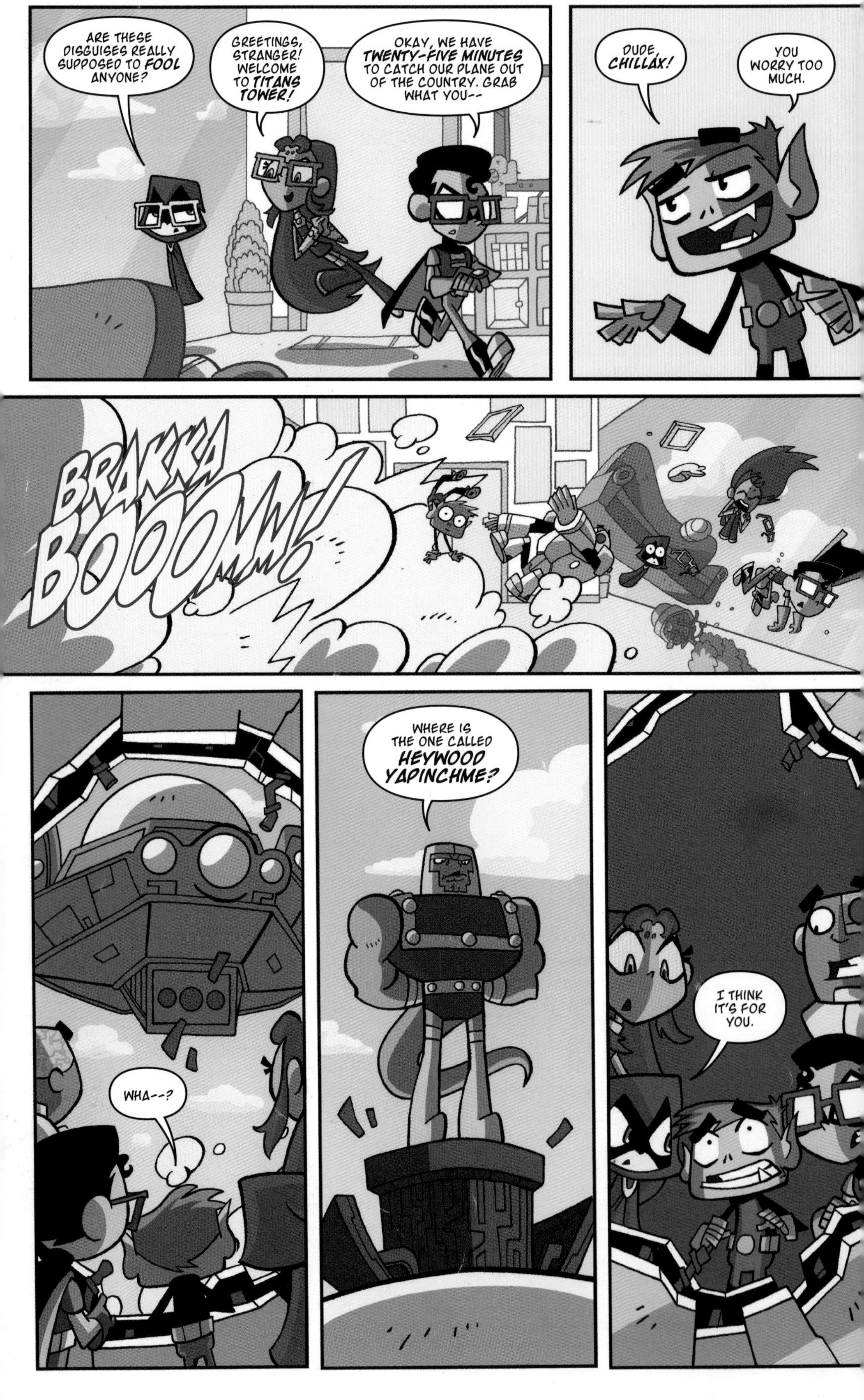

ARE THESE DISGUISES REALLY SUPPOSED TO FOOL ANYONE?
GREETINGS, STRANGER! WELCOME TO TITANS TOWER!
OKAY, WE HAVE TWENTY-FIVE MINUTES TO CATCH OUR PLANE OUT OF THE COUNTRY. GRAB WHAT YOU--
DUDE, CHILLAX!
YOU WORRY TOO MUCH.
BRAKKA BOOOOM!!
WHA--?
WHERE IS THE ONE CALLED HEYWOOD YAPINCHME?
I THINK IT'S FOR YOU.

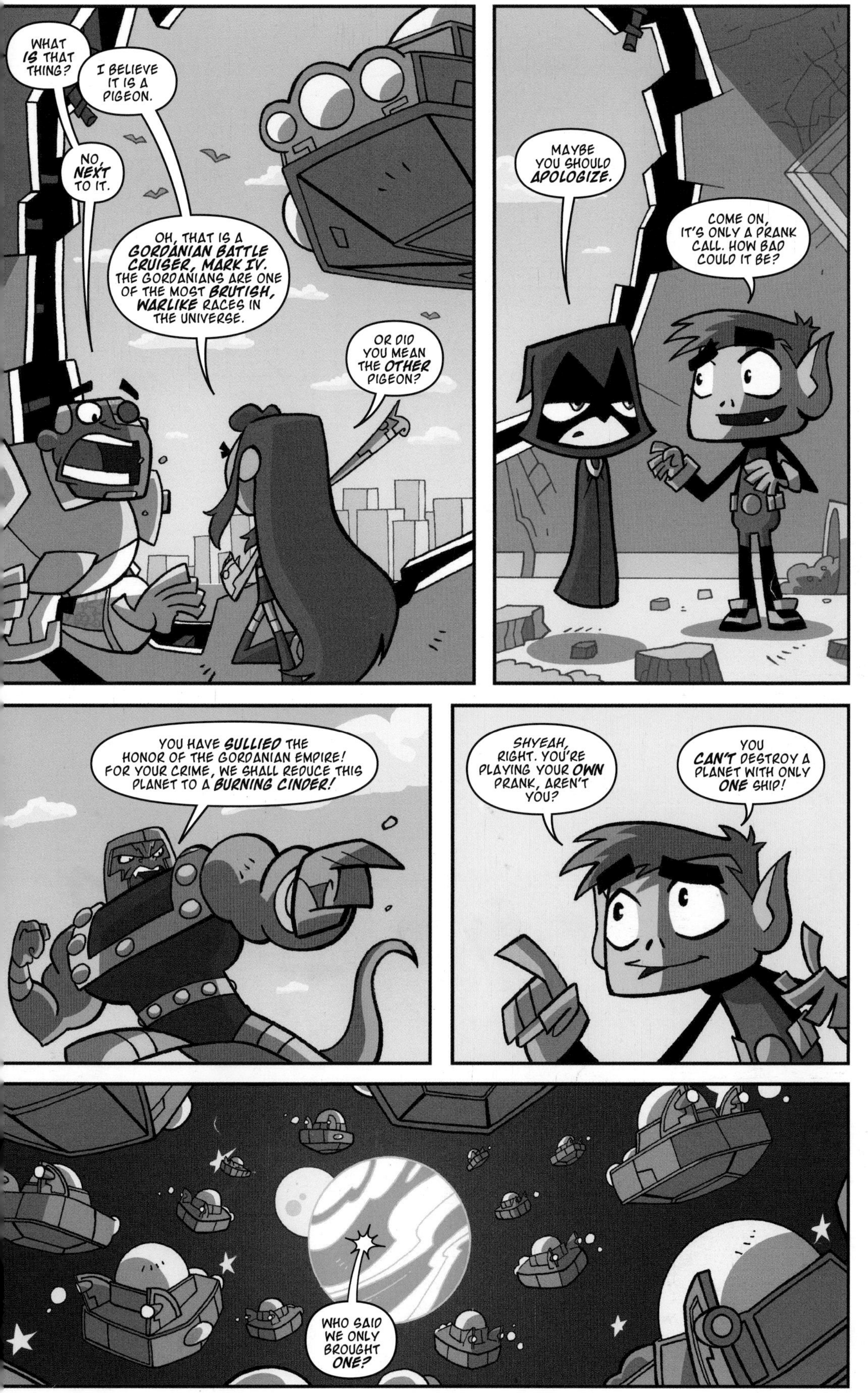
WHAT IS THAT THING?
I BELIEVE IT IS A PIGEON.
NO, NEXT TO IT.
OH, THAT IS A GORDANIAN BATTLE CRUISER, MARK IV. THE GORDANIANS ARE ONE OF THE MOST BRUTISH, WARLIKE RACES IN THE UNIVERSE.
OR DID YOU MEAN THE OTHER PIGEON?
MAYBE YOU SHOULD APOLOGIZE.
COME ON, IT'S ONLY A PRANK CALL. HOW BAD COULD IT BE?
YOU HAVE SULLIED THE HONOR OF THE GORDANIAN EMPIRE! FOR YOUR CRIME, WE SHALL REDUCE THIS PLANET TO A BURNING CINDER!
SHYEAH, RIGHT. YOU'RE PLAYING YOUR OWN PRANK, AREN'T YOU?
YOU CAN'T DESTROY A PLANET WITH ONLY ONE SHIP!
WHO SAID WE ONLY BROUGHT ONE?

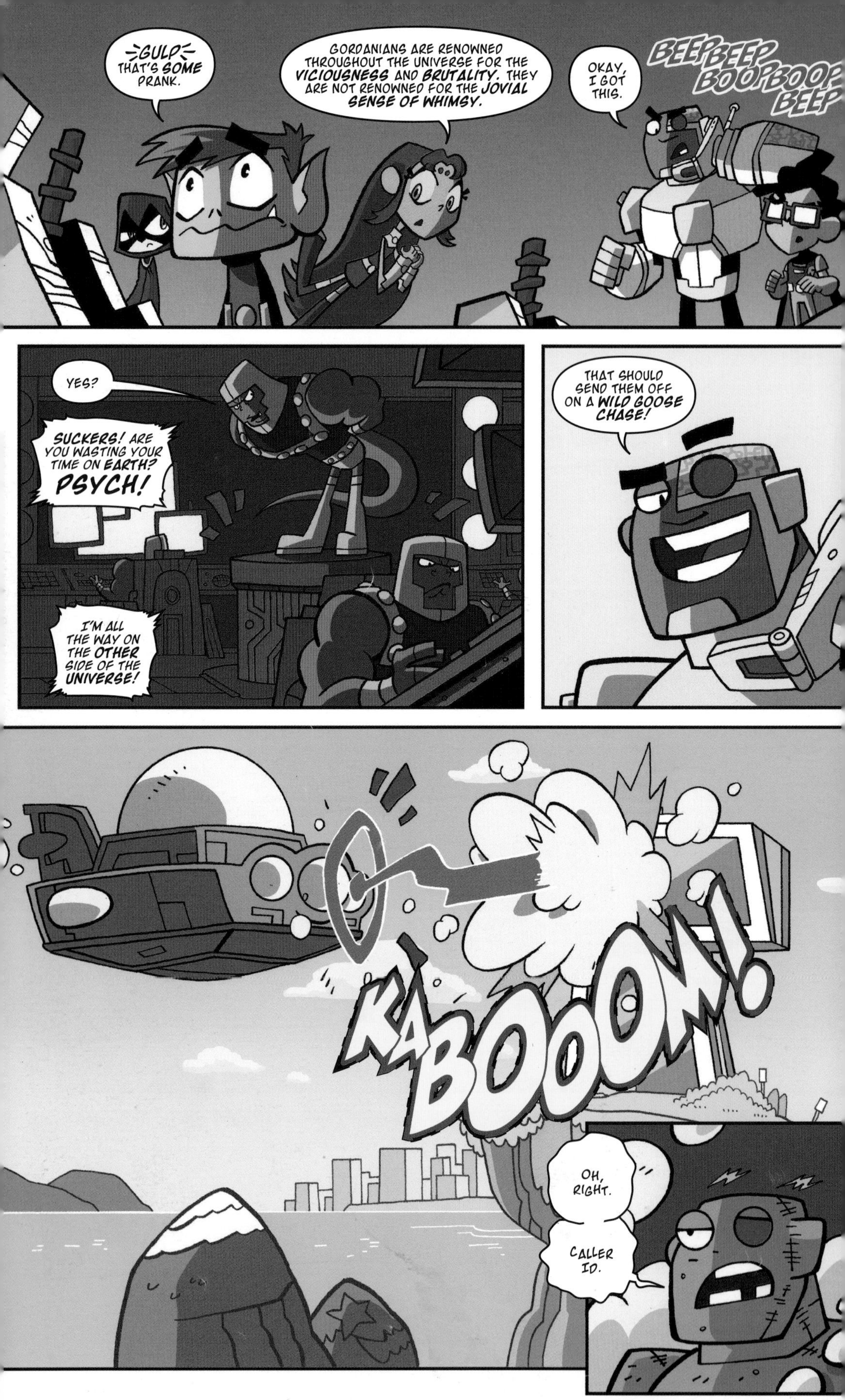

GULP
THAT'S SOME PRANK.
GORDANIANS ARE RENOWNED THROUGHOUT THE UNIVERSE FOR THE VICIOUSNESS AND BRUTALITY. THEY ARE NOT RENOWNED FOR THE JOVIAL SENSE OF WHIMSY.
OKAY, I GOT THIS.
BEEP BEEP BOOP BOOP BEEP
YES?
SUCKERS! ARE YOU WASTING YOUR TIME ON EARTH? PSYCH!
I'M ALL THE WAY ON THE OTHER SIDE OF THE UNIVERSE!
THAT SHOULD SEND THEM OFF ON A WILD GOOSE CHASE!
KABOOOM!
OH, RIGHT.
CALLER ID.

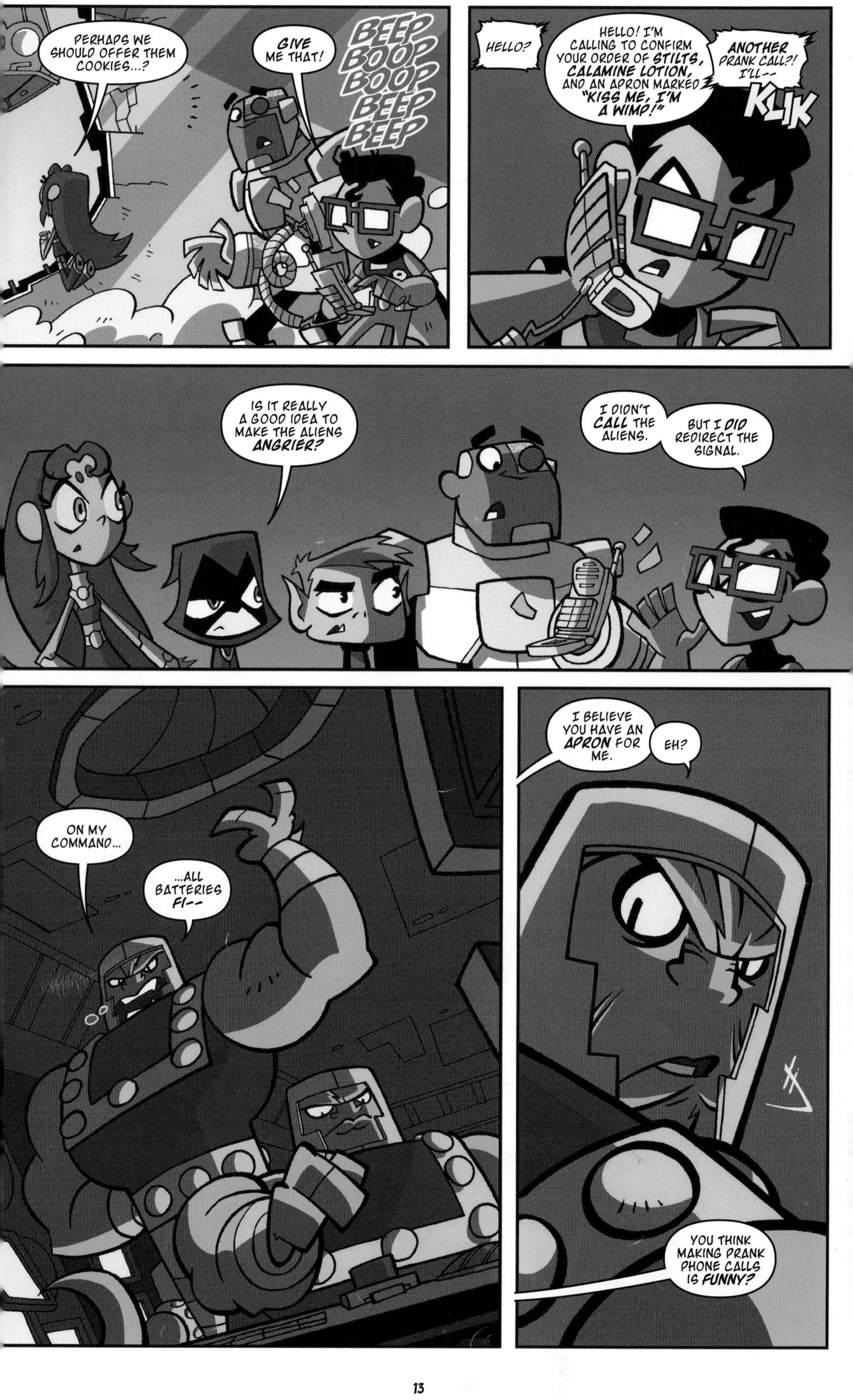
PERHAPS WE SHOULD OFFER THEM COOKIES...?
GIVE ME THAT!
BEEP BOOP BOOP BEEP BEEP
HELLO?
HELLO! I'M CALLING TO CONFIRM YOUR ORDER OF STILTS, CALAMINE LOTION, AND AN APRON MARKED "KISS ME, I'M A WIMP!"
ANOTHER PRANK CALL?! I'LL--
KLIK
IS IT REALLY A GOOD IDEA TO MAKE THE ALIENS ANGRIER?
I DIDN'T CALL THE ALIENS.
BUT I DID REDIRECT THE SIGNAL.
ON MY COMMAND...
...ALL BATTERIES FI--
I BELIEVE YOU HAVE AN APRON FOR ME.
EH?
YOU THINK MAKING PRANK PHONE CALLS IS FUNNY?

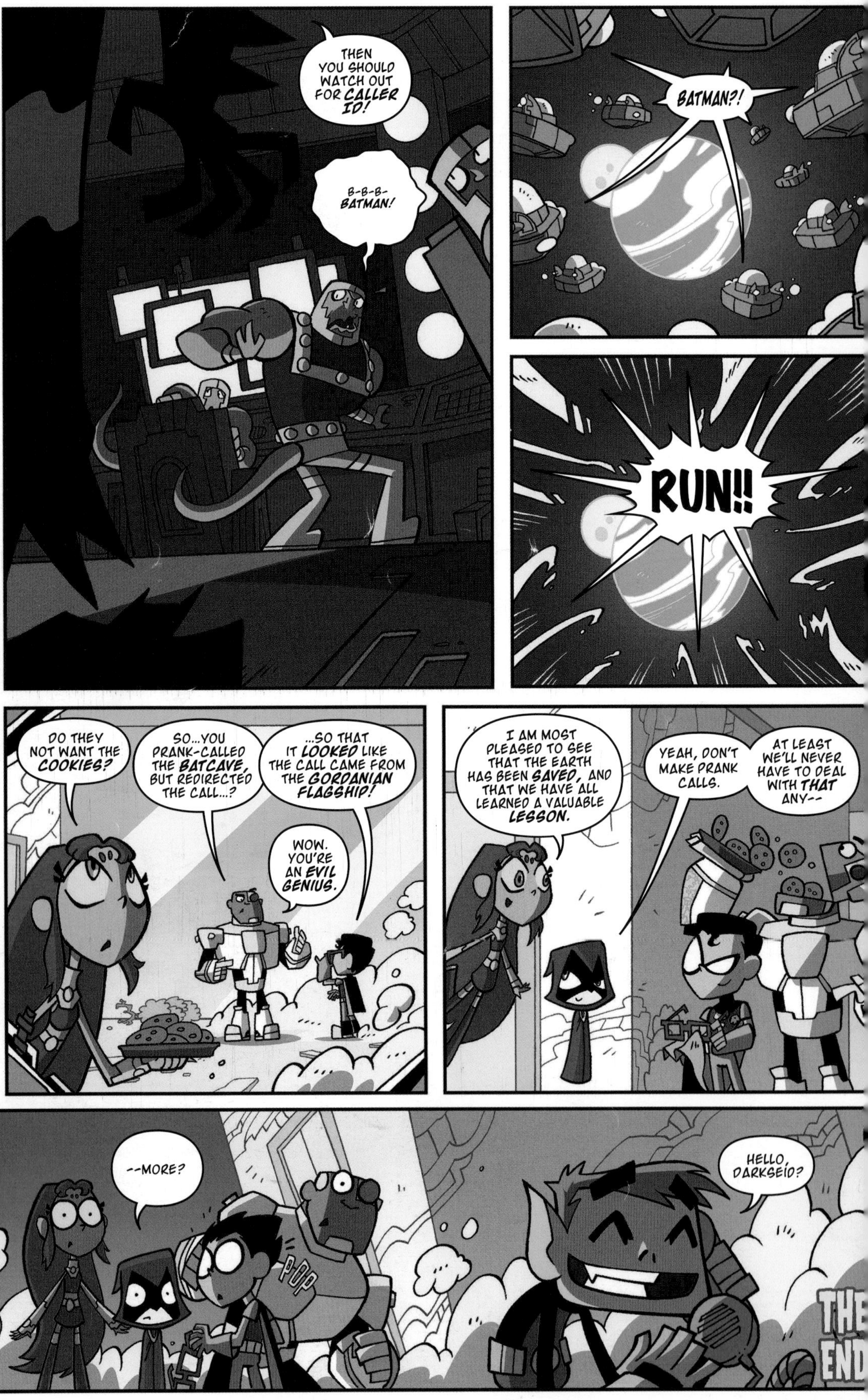
THEN YOU SHOULD WATCH OUT FOR CALLER ID!
B-B-B-BATMAN!
BATMAN?!
RUN!!
DO THEY NOT WANT THE COOKIES?
SO...YOU PRANK-CALLED THE BATCAVE, BUT REDIRECTED THE CALL...?
...SO THAT IT LOOKED LIKE THE CALL CAME FROM THE GORDANIAN FLAGSHIP!
WOW. YOU'RE AN EVIL GENIUS.
I AM MOST PLEASED TO SEE THAT THE EARTH HAS BEEN SAVED, AND THAT WE HAVE ALL LEARNED A VALUABLE LESSON.
YEAH, DON'T MAKE PRANK CALLS.
AT LEAST WE'LL NEVER HAVE TO DEAL WITH THAT ANY--
--MORE?
HELLO, DARKSEID?
THE END

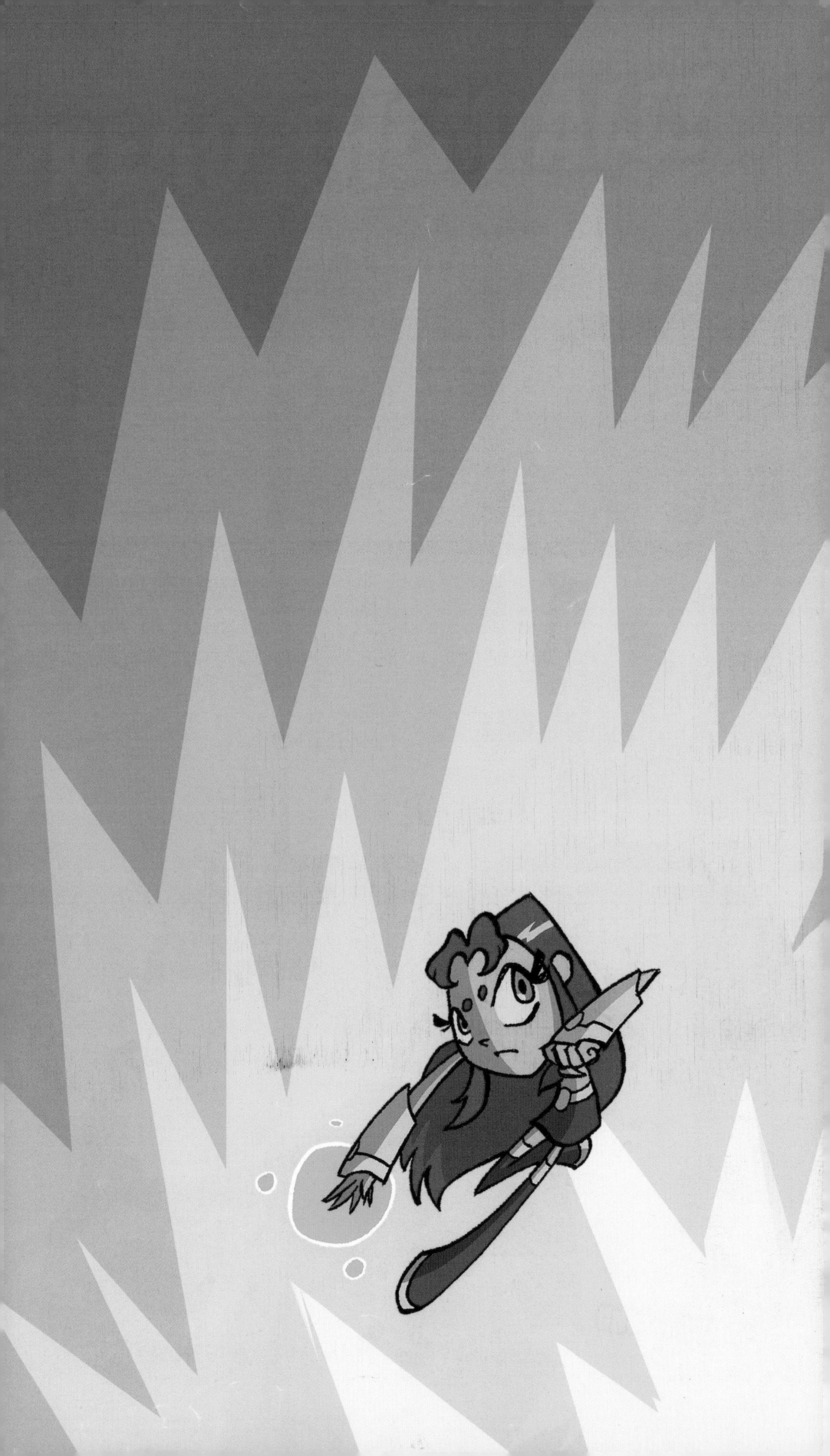

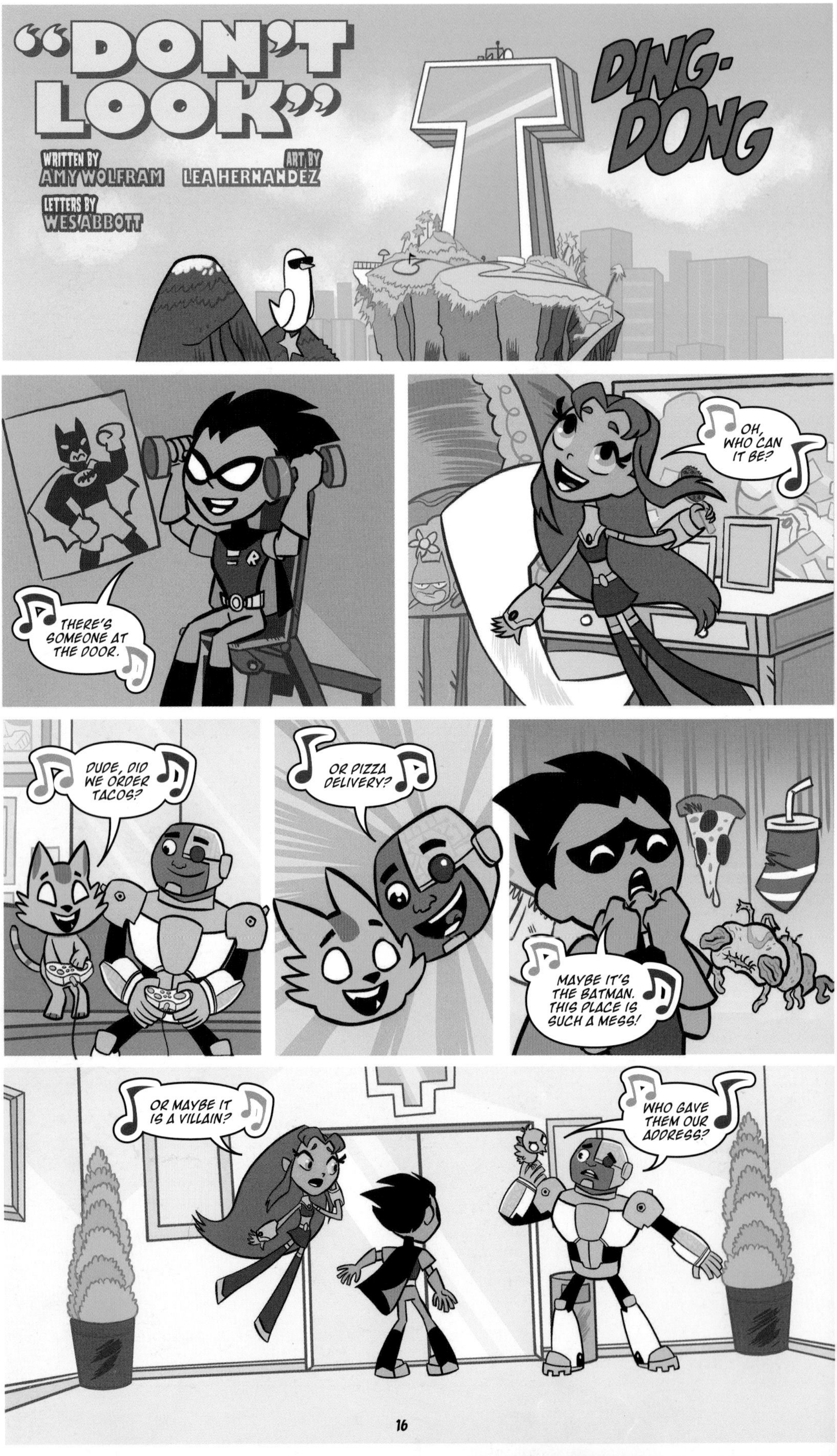
"DON'T LOOK"
WRITTEN BY AMY WOLFRAM
ART BY LEA HERNANDEZ
LETTERS BY WES ABBOTT
DING-DONG
THERE'S SOMEONE AT THE DOOR.
OH, WHO CAN IT BE?
DUDE, DID WE ORDER TACOS?
OR PIZZA DELIVERY?
MAYBE IT'S THE BATMAN. THIS PLACE IS SUCH A MESS!
OR MAYBE IT IS A VILLAIN?
WHO GAVE THEM OUR ADDRESS?

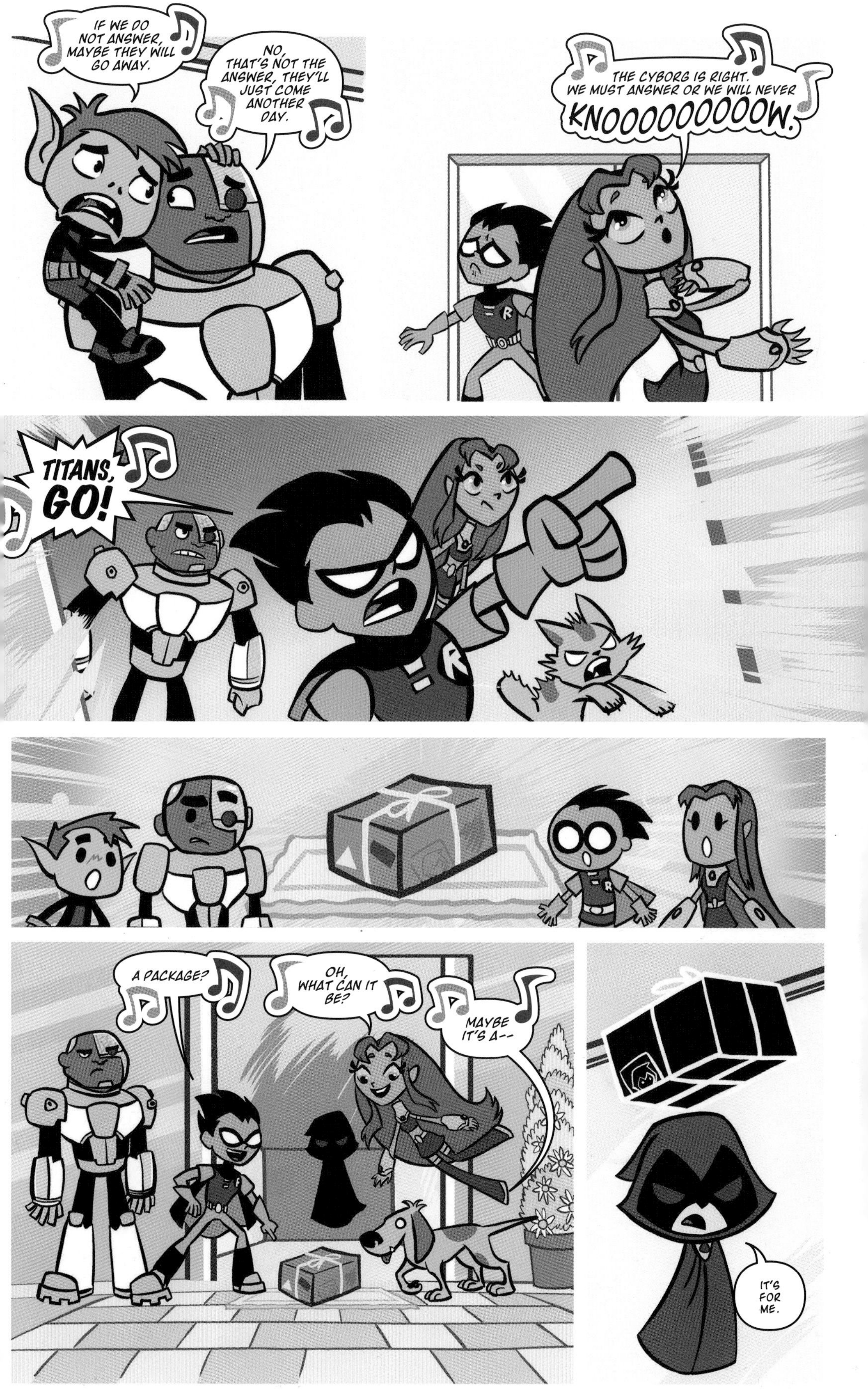
IF WE DO NOT ANSWER, MAYBE THEY WILL GO AWAY.
NO, THAT'S NOT THE ANSWER, THEY'LL JUST COME ANOTHER DAY.
THE CYBORG IS RIGHT. WE MUST ANSWER OR WE WILL NEVER KNOOOOOOOOOW.
TITANS, GO!
A PACKAGE?
OH, WHAT CAN IT BE?
MAYBE IT'S A--
IT'S FOR ME.

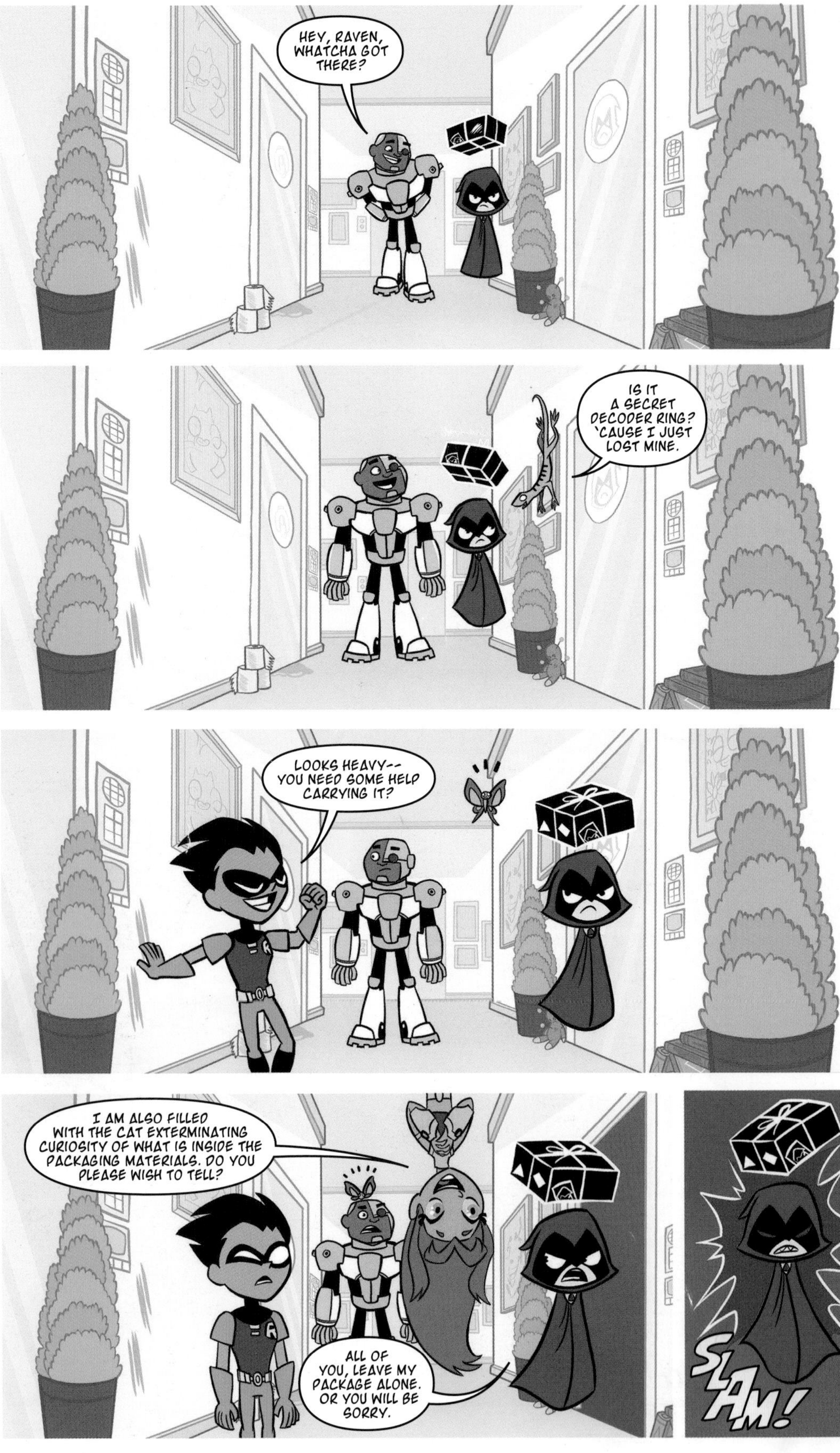
HEY, RAVEN, WHATCHA GOT THERE?
IS IT A SECRET DECODER RING? 'CAUSE I JUST LOST MINE.
LOOKS HEAVY-- YOU NEED SOME HELP CARRYING IT?
I AM ALSO FILLED WITH THE CAT EXTERMINATING CURIOSITY OF WHAT IS INSIDE THE PACKAGING MATERIALS. DO YOU PLEASE WISH TO TELL?
ALL OF YOU, LEAVE MY PACKAGE ALONE. OR YOU WILL BE SORRY.
SLAM!

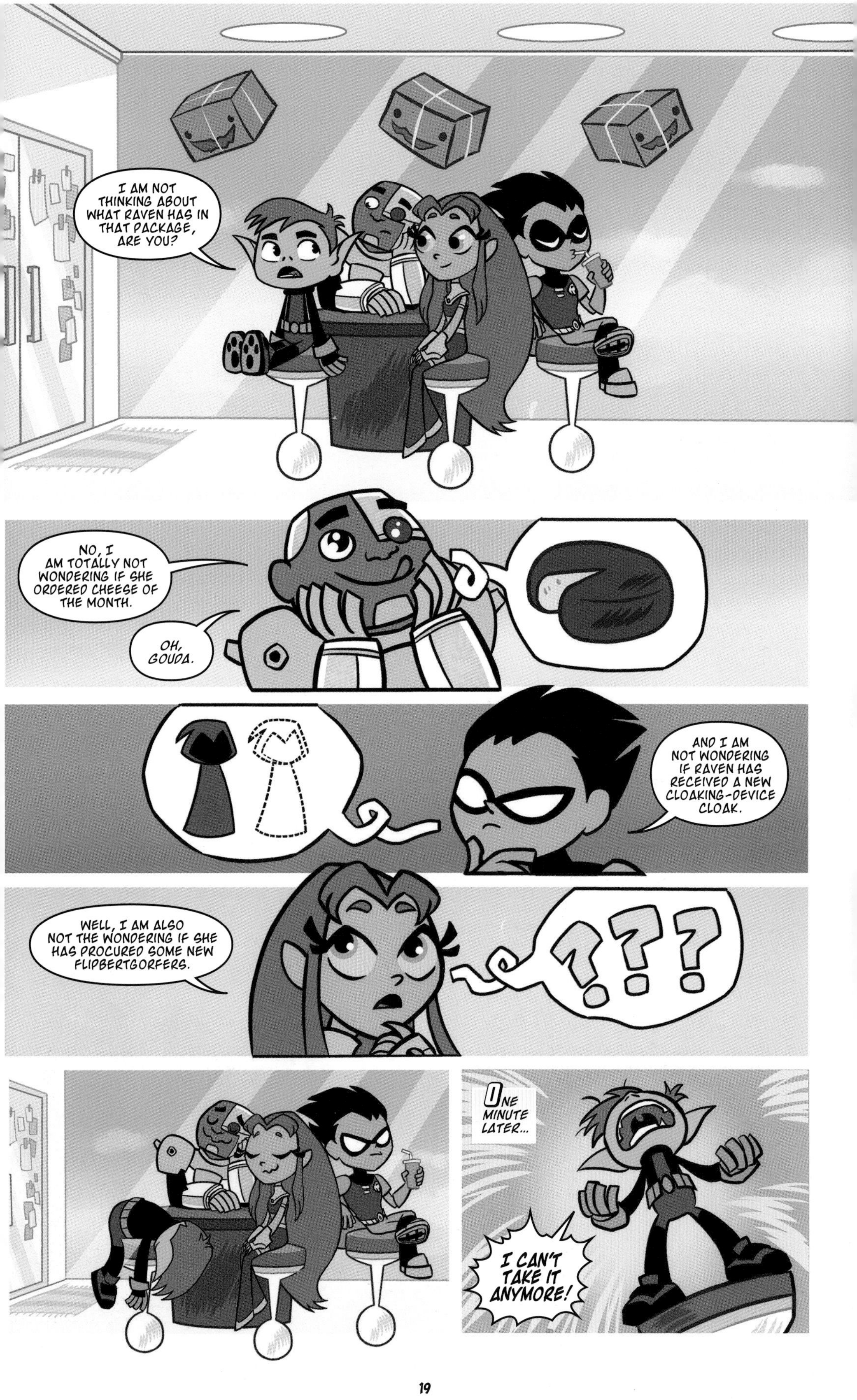

I AM NOT THINKING ABOUT WHAT RAVEN HAS IN THAT PACKAGE, ARE YOU?
NO, I AM TOTALLY NOT WONDERING IF SHE ORDERED CHEESE OF THE MONTH.
OH, GOUDA.
AND I AM NOT WONDERING IF RAVEN HAS RECEIVED A NEW CLOAKING-DEVICE CLOAK.
WELL, I AM ALSO NOT THE WONDERING IF SHE HAS PROCURED SOME NEW FLIPBERTGORFERS.
???
ONE MINUTE LATER...
I CAN'T TAKE IT ANYMORE!

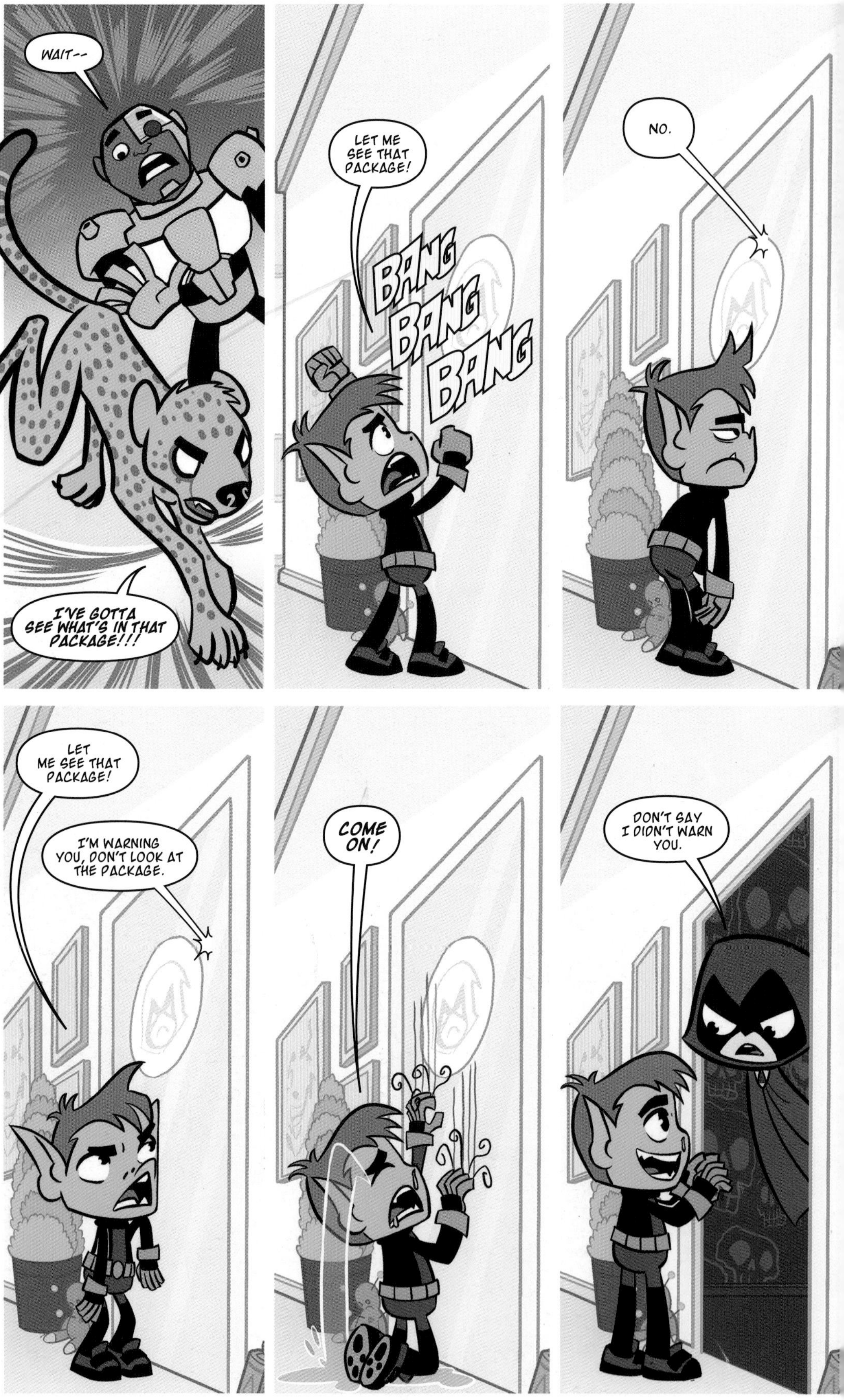

WAIT--
I'VE GOTTA SEE WHAT'S IN THAT PACKAGE!!!
LET ME SEE THAT PACKAGE!
BANG BANG BANG
NO.
LET ME SEE THAT PACKAGE!
I'M WARNING YOU, DON'T LOOK AT THE PACKAGE.
COME ON!
DON'T SAY I DIDN'T WARN YOU.

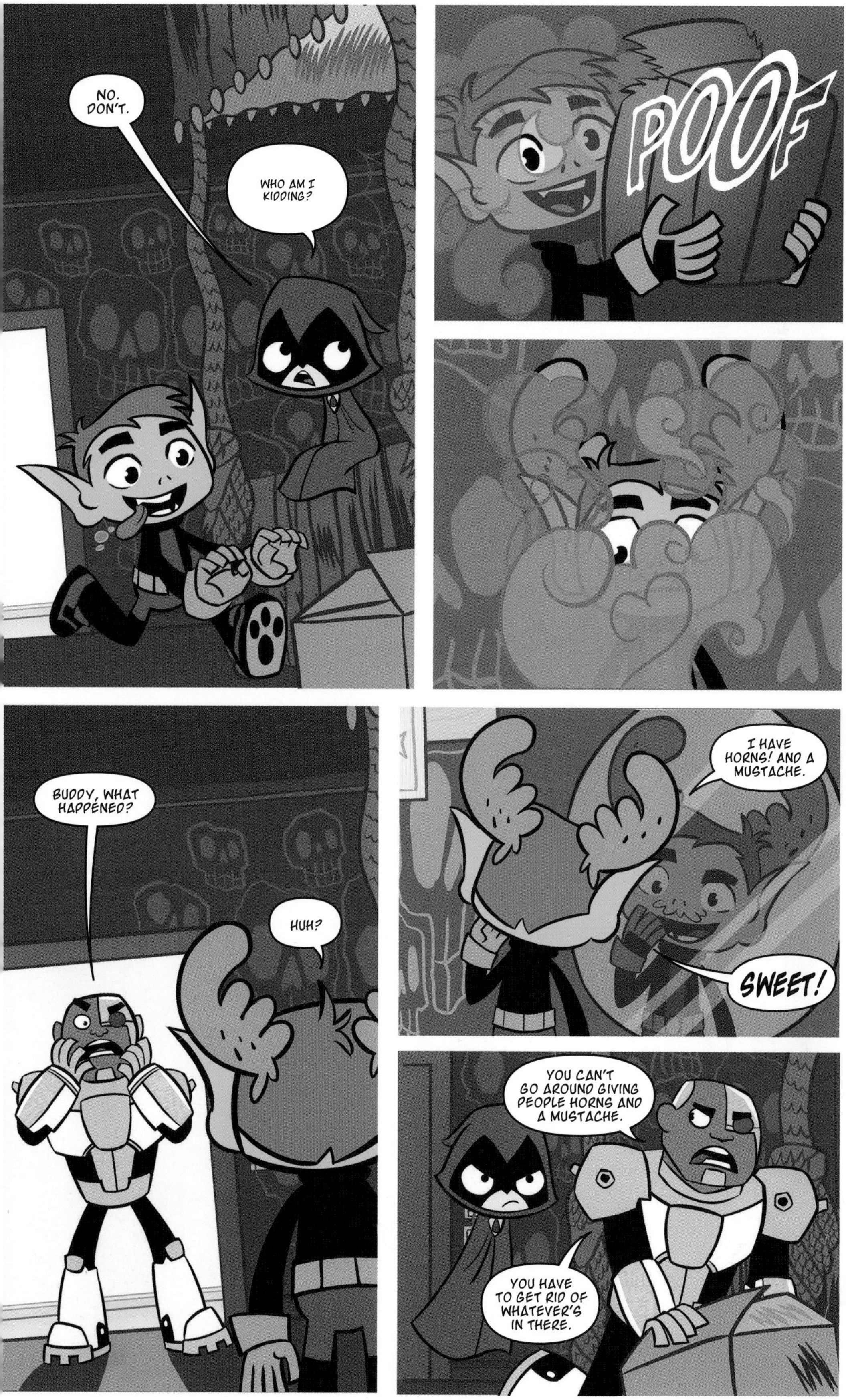

NO. DON'T.
WHO AM I KIDDING?
POOF
BUDDY, WHAT HAPPENED?
HUH?
I HAVE HORNS! AND A MUSTACHE.
SWEET!
YOU CAN'T GO AROUND GIVING PEOPLE HORNS AND A MUSTACHE.
YOU HAVE TO GET RID OF WHATEVER'S IN THERE.

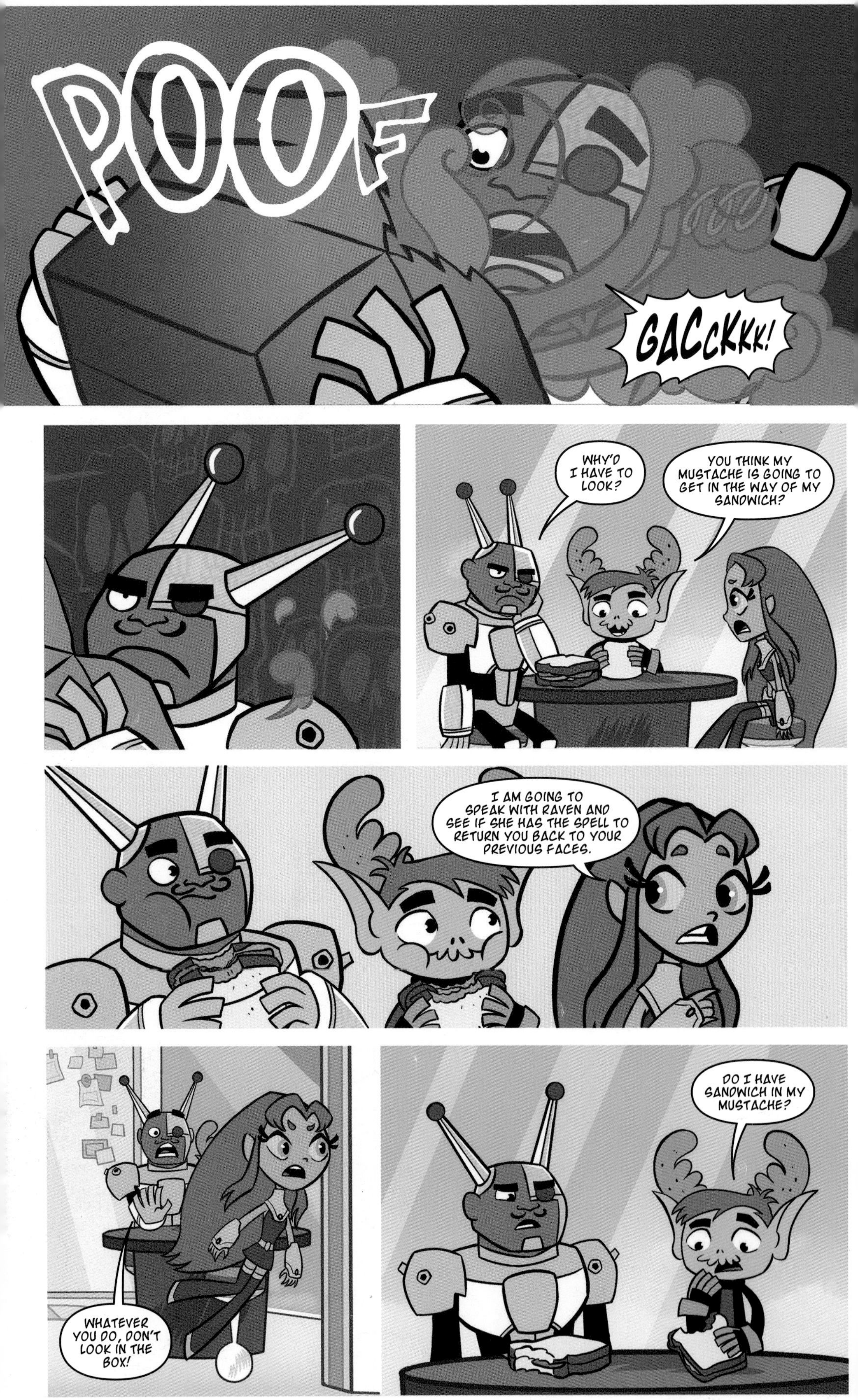
POOF
GACCKKK!
WHY'D I HAVE TO LOOK?
YOU THINK MY MUSTACHE IS GOING TO GET IN THE WAY OF MY SANDWICH?
I AM GOING TO SPEAK WITH RAVEN AND SEE IF SHE HAS THE SPELL TO RETURN YOU BACK TO YOUR PREVIOUS FACES.
WHATEVER YOU DO, DON'T LOOK IN THE BOX!
DO I HAVE SANDWICH IN MY MUSTACHE?

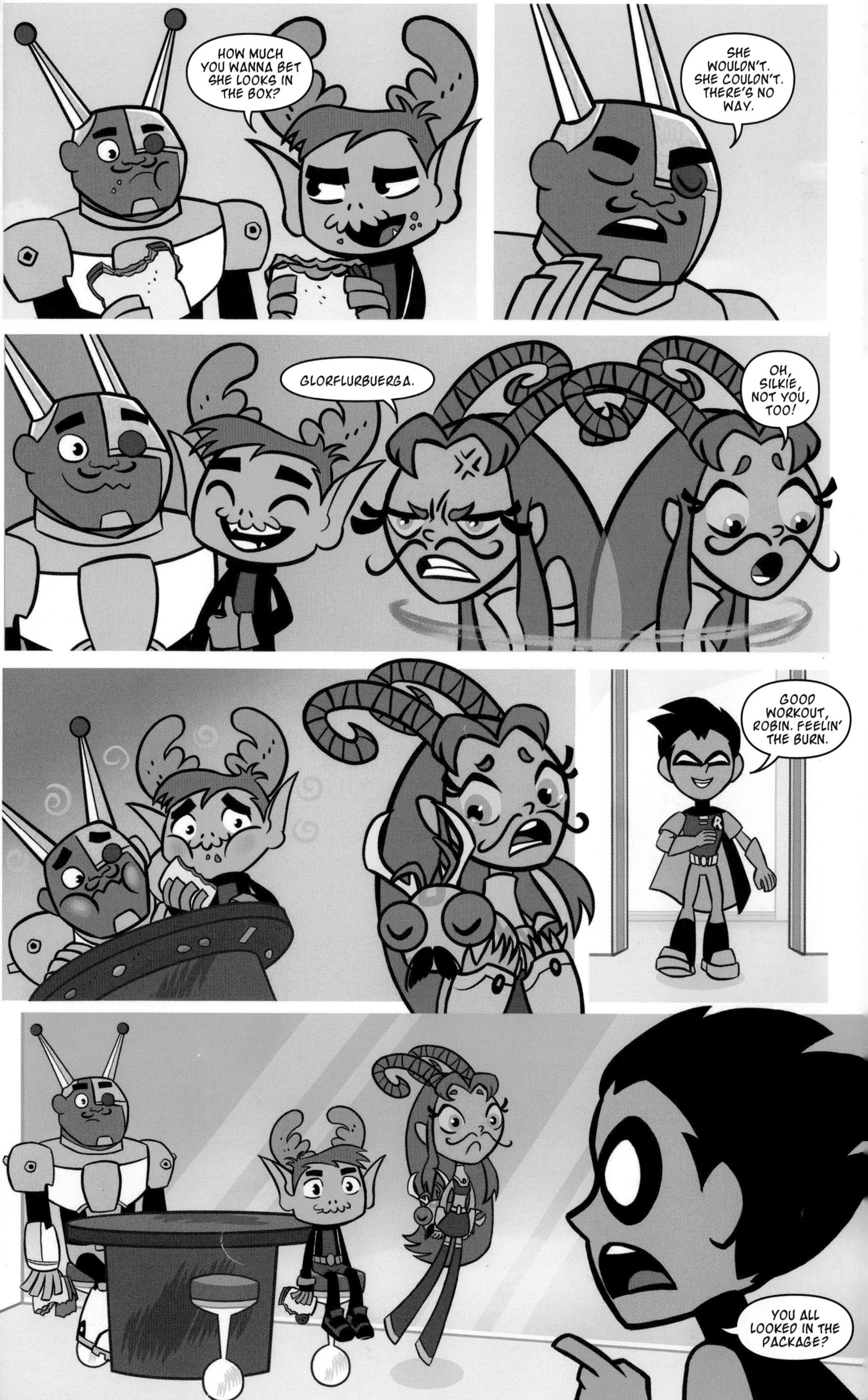
HOW MUCH YOU WANNA BET SHE LOOKS IN THE BOX?
SHE WOULDN'T. SHE COULDN'T. THERE'S NO WAY.
GLORFLURBUERGA.
OH, SILKIE, NOT YOU, TOO!
GOOD WORKOUT, ROBIN. FEELIN' THE BURN.
YOU ALL LOOKED IN THE PACKAGE?

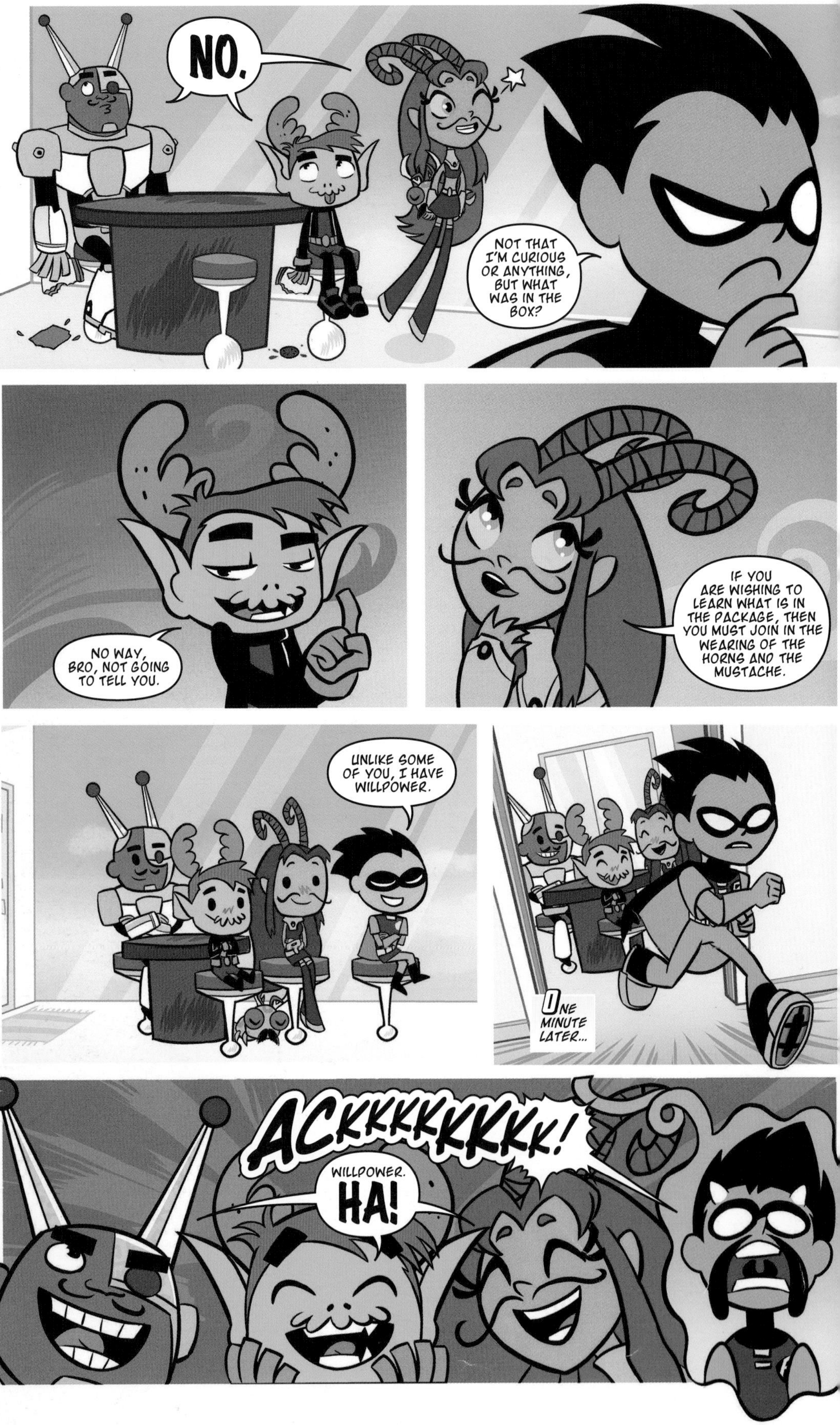

NO.
NOT THAT I'M CURIOUS OR ANYTHING, BUT WHAT WAS IN THE BOX?
NO WAY, BRO, NOT GOING TO TELL YOU.
IF YOU ARE WISHING TO LEARN WHAT IS IN THE PACKAGE, THEN YOU MUST JOIN IN THE WEARING OF THE HORNS AND THE MUSTACHE.
UNLIKE SOME OF YOU, I HAVE WILLPOWER.
ONE MINUTE LATER...
ACKKKKKKKK!
WILLPOWER. HA!

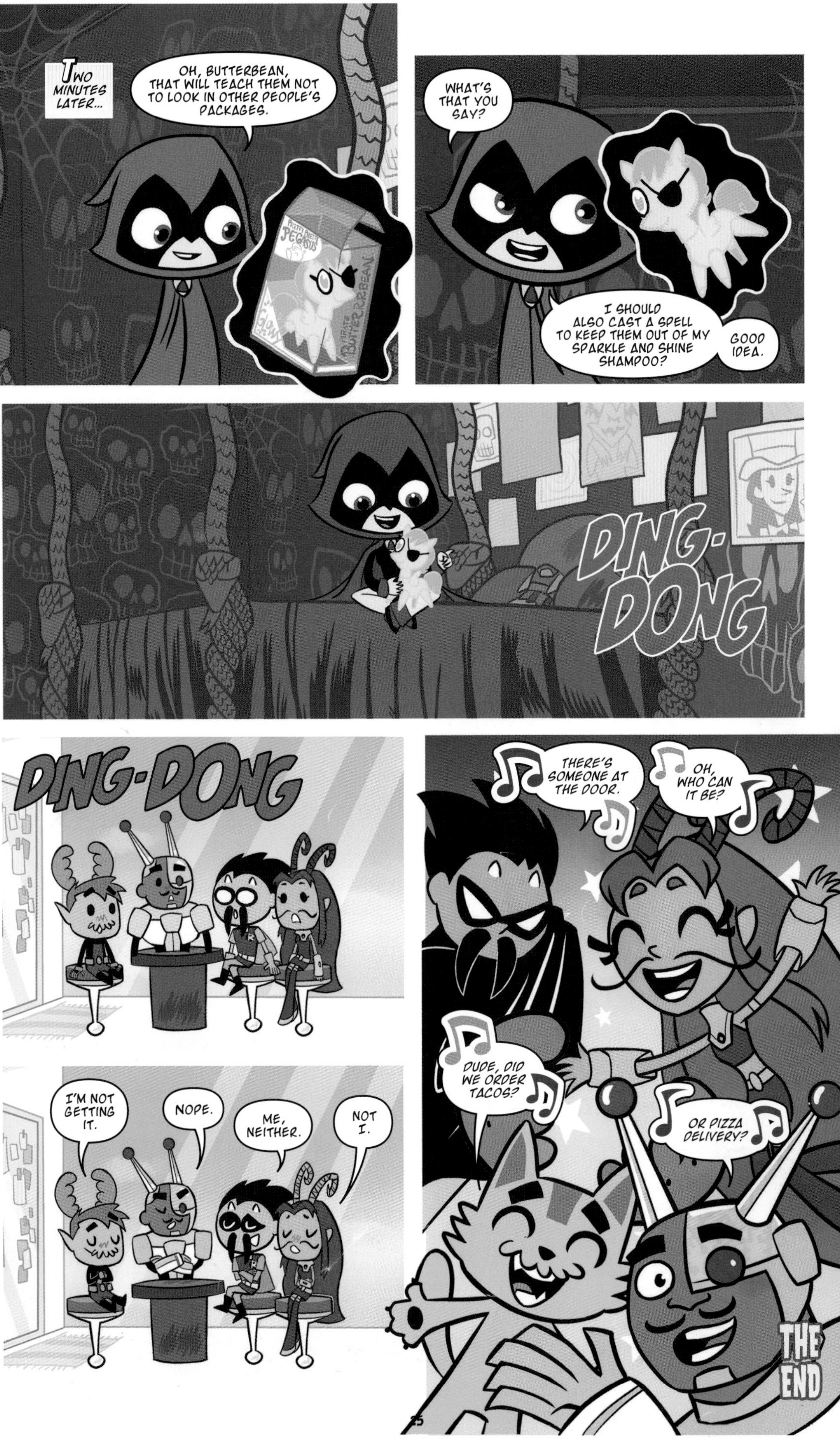
TWO MINUTES LATER...
OH, BUTTERBEAN, THAT WILL TEACH THEM NOT TO LOOK IN OTHER PEOPLE'S PACKAGES.
PRETTY PRETTY PEGASUS
PIRATE BUTTERBEAN
WHAT'S THAT YOU SAY?
I SHOULD ALSO CAST A SPELL TO KEEP THEM OUT OF MY SPARKLE AND SHINE SHAMPOO?
GOOD IDEA.
DING-DONG
DING-DONG
I'M NOT GETTING IT.
NOPE.
ME, NEITHER.
NOT I.
THERE'S SOMEONE AT THE DOOR.
OH, WHO CAN IT BE?
DUDE, DID WE ORDER TACOS?
OR PIZZA DELIVERY?
THE END

CREATORS

SHOLLY FISCH

Bitten by a radioactive typewriter, Sholly Fisch has spent the wee hours writing books, comics, TV scripts, and online material for over 25 years. His comic book credits include more than 200 stories and features about characters such as Batman, Superman, Bugs Bunny, Daffy Duck, Spider-Man, and Ben 10. Currently, he writes stories for Action Comics every month, plus stories for Looney Tunes and Scooby-Doo. By day, Sholly is a mild-mannered developmental psychologist who helps to create educational TV shows, web sites, and other media for kids.

AMY WOLFRAM

Amy Wolfram is a comic book and television writer. She has written episodes for the animated TV series *Teen Titans*, *Legion of Super-Heroes*, and *Teen Titans Go!*. In addition to the *Teen Titans Go!* comic book series, she has also written for *Teen Titans: Year One*.

JORGE CORONA

Jorge Corona is a Venezuelan comic artist who is well-known for his all-ages fantasy-adventure series *Feathers* and his work on *Jim Henson's The Storyteller: Dragons*. In addition to *Teen Titans Go!*, he has also worked on *Batman Beyond*, *Justice League Beyond*, *We Are Robin*, *Goners*, and many other comics.

LEA HERNANDEZ

Lea Hernandez is a comic book artist and webcomic creator who is known for her manga-influenced style. She has worked with Marvel Comics, Oni Press, NBM Publishing, and DC Comics. In addition to her work on *Teen Titans Go!*, she is the co-creator of *Killer Princesses* and the creator of *Rumble Girls*.

GLOSSARY

brutality (broo-TAL-uh-tee)—being cruel and violent

brutish (BROOT-ish)—rough and violent

cinder (SIN-duhr)—a piece of wood or other material that has been burned up

confirm (kuhn-FURM)—to make sure something is definitely true or will happen

continent (KAHN-tuh-nuhnt)—one of Earth's seven large land masses

cosmic (KAHZ-mik)—having to do with outer space, the universe, or the heavens

evacuation (i-vak-yoo-AY-shuhn)—movement away from an area because it is dangerous

exterminate (ik-STUHR-muh-nayt)—to wipe out or destroy

galaxy (GAL-uhk-see)—cluster of millions of stars bound together by gravity

hysterical (hi-STER-uh-kuhl)—extremely funny

insult (IN-sult)—a hurtful remark

jovial (JO-vee-uhl)—happy

originate (uh-RIJ-uh-nate)—to begin from somewhere or something

procure (pro-KYOOR)—to get or obtain

rapier (RAY-pee-ur)—sharp, like the two edges of the rapier sword

renowned (ri-NOUND)—well-known or famous

satellite (SAT-uh-lite)—a spacecraft used to send signals and information from one place to another

sully (SUHL-ee)—to make dirty or damage

tradition (truh-DISH-uhn)—a custom, idea, or belief passed down through time

transmission (transs-MISH-uhn)—a signal or message that is sent from one place to another

untraceable (uhn-TRAYSS-uh-bul)—unable to be followed back to its source

viciousness (VISH-uhss-ness)—being fierce or dangerous

whimsy (WIM-zee)—playful or fanciful behavior

willpower (WIL-pou-ur)—strong determination

VISUAL QUESTIONS & WRITING PROMPTS

1. What super hero are the Teen Titans mimicking with their disguises? What details in the panel help you know?

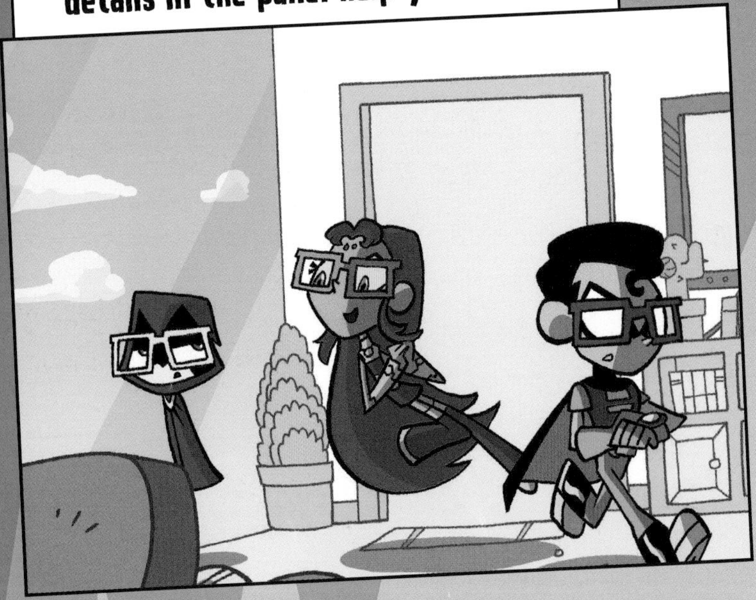

2. At the end of the first story, Beast Boy is about to prank call the super-villain Darkseid. Write a short story about what happens next.

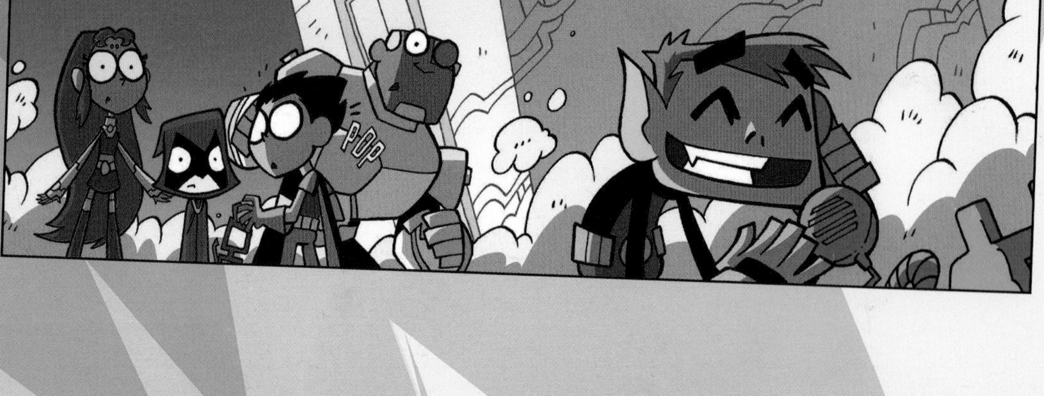
POP

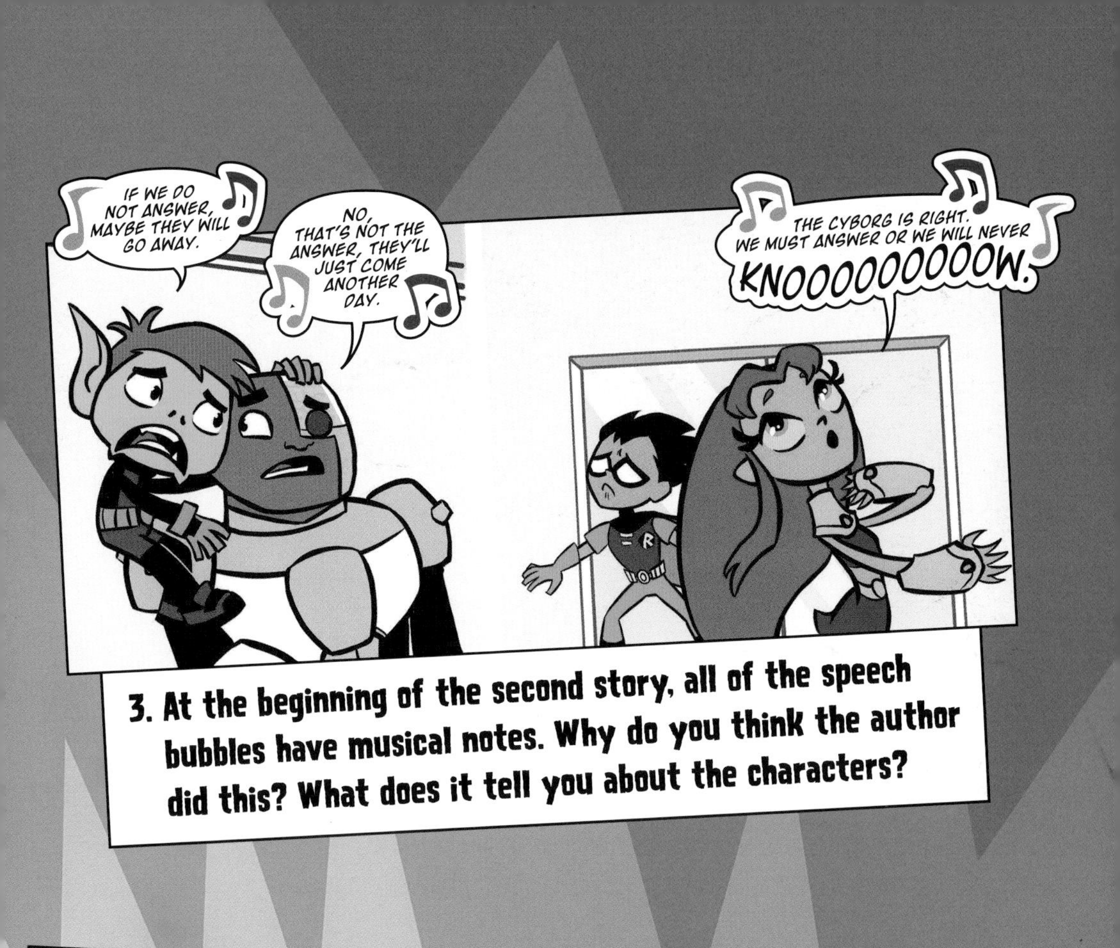
IF WE DO NOT ANSWER, MAYBE THEY WILL GO AWAY.
NO, THAT'S NOT THE ANSWER, THEY'LL JUST COME ANOTHER DAY.
THE CYBORG IS RIGHT. WE MUST ANSWER OR WE WILL NEVER KNOOOOOOOOOW.

3. At the beginning of the second story, all of the speech bubbles have musical notes. Why do you think the author did this? What does it tell you about the characters?

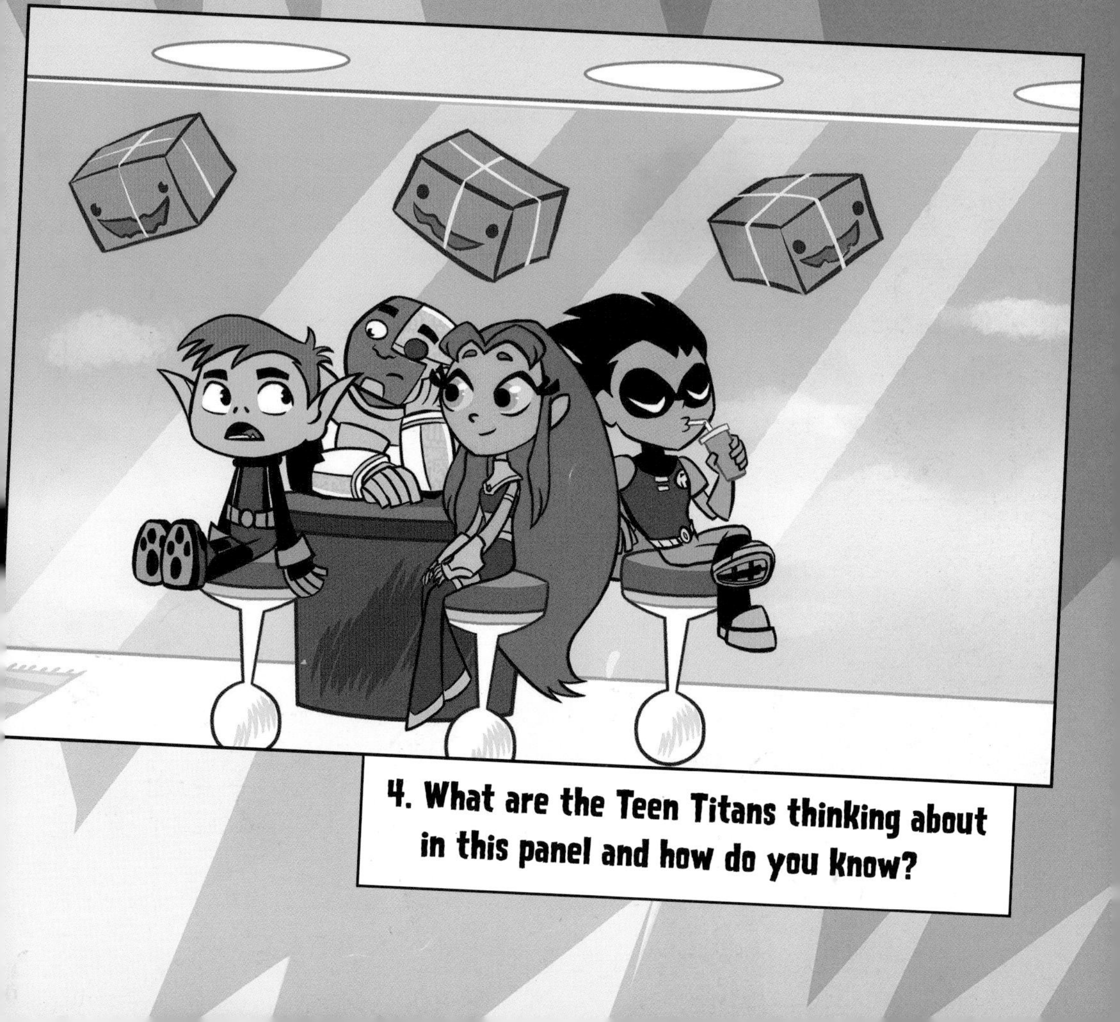

4. What are the Teen Titans thinking about in this panel and how do you know?

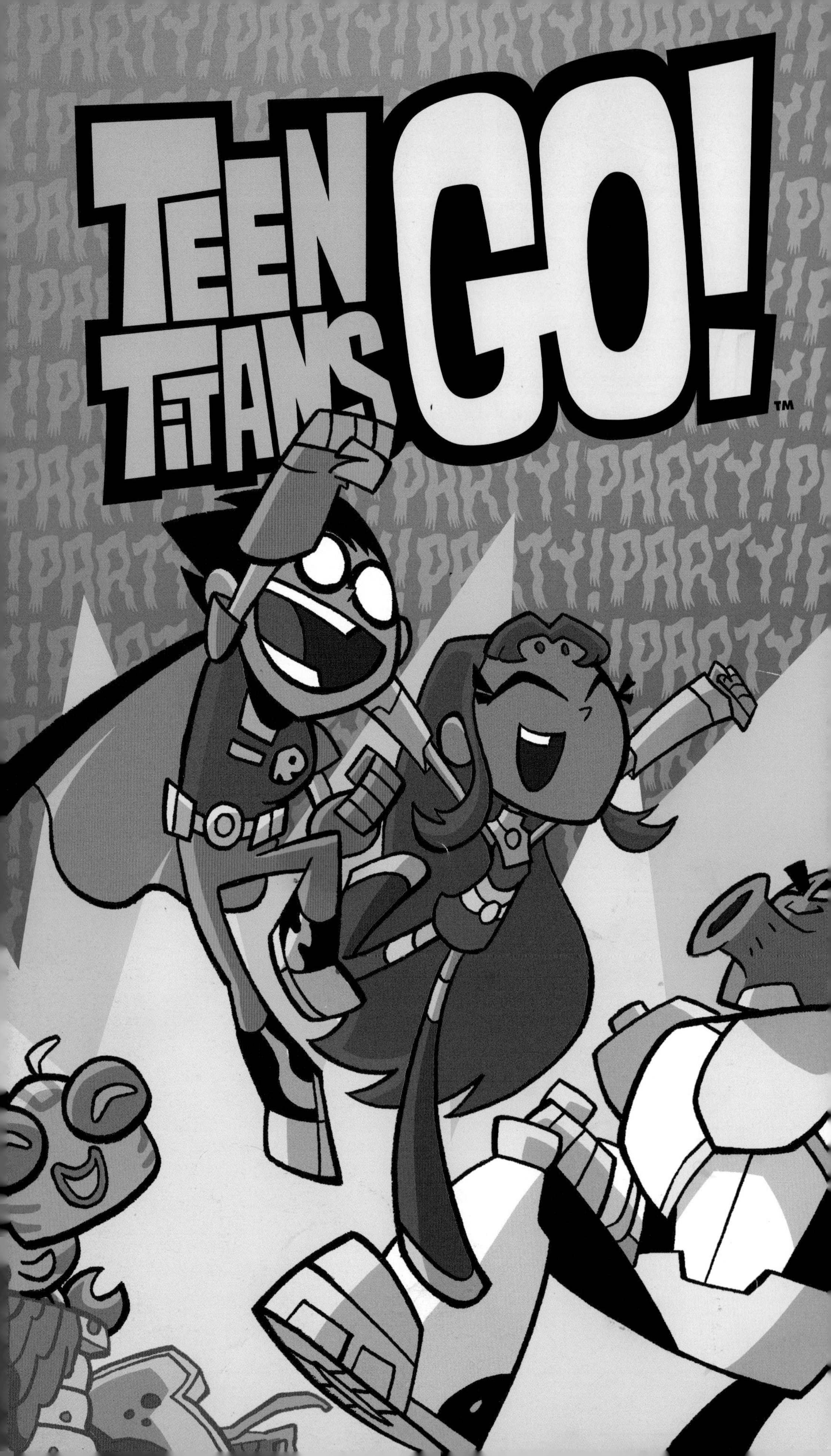

TEEN TITANS GO!™
PARTY! PARTY! PARTY!

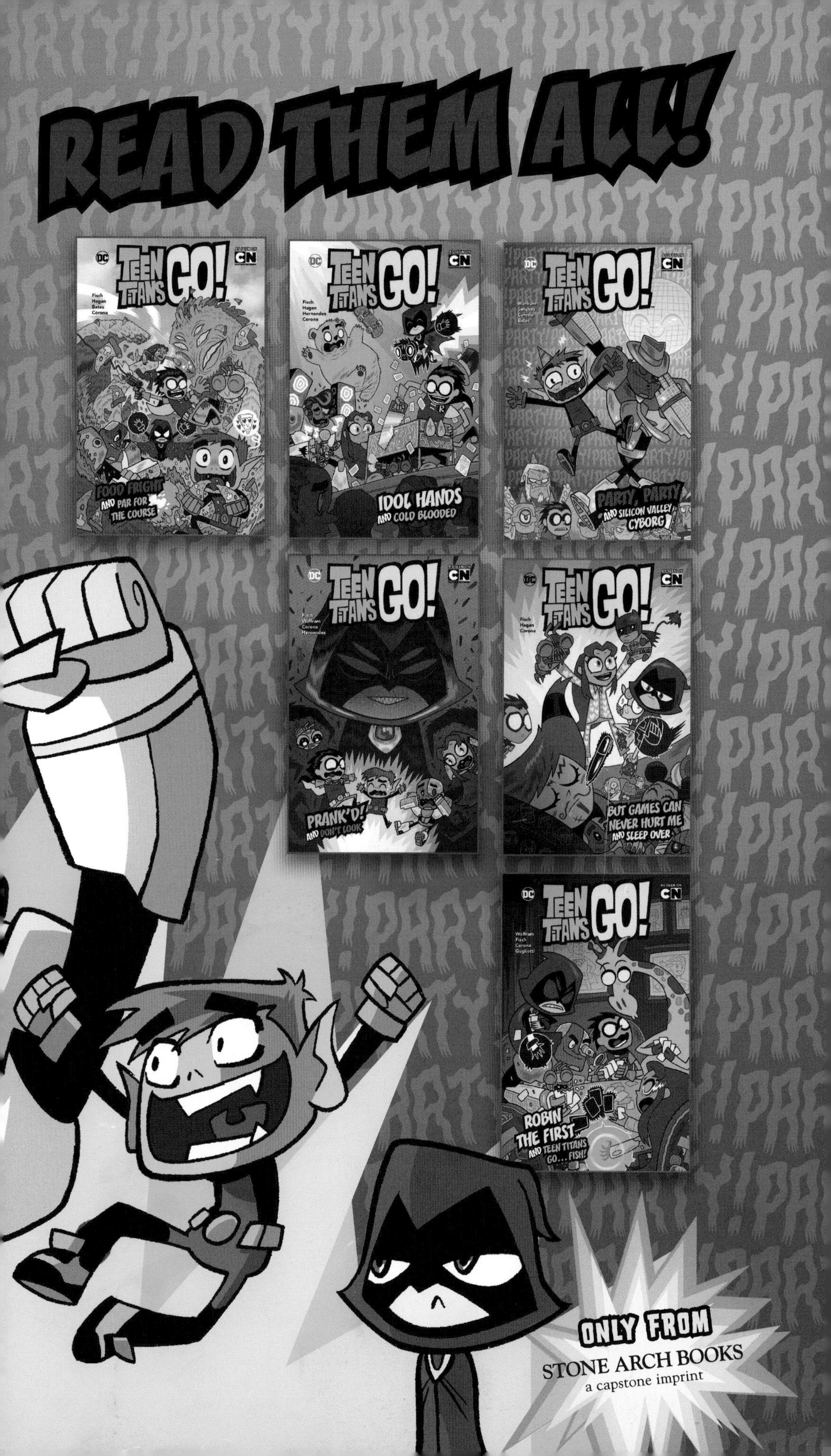
READ THEM ALL!
TEEN TITANS GO!
FOOD FRIGHT AND PAR FOR THE COURSE
TEEN TITANS GO!
IDOL HANDS AND COLD BLOODED
TEEN TITANS GO!
PARTY, PARTY AND SILICON VALLEY CYBORG
TEEN TITANS GO!
PRANK'D! AND DON'T LOOK
TEEN TITANS GO!
BUT GAMES CAN NEVER HURT ME AND SLEEP OVER
TEEN TITANS GO!
ROBIN THE FIRST AND TEEN TITANS GO... FISH!
ONLY FROM
STONE ARCH BOOKS
a capstone imprint

TEEN TITANS GO!™

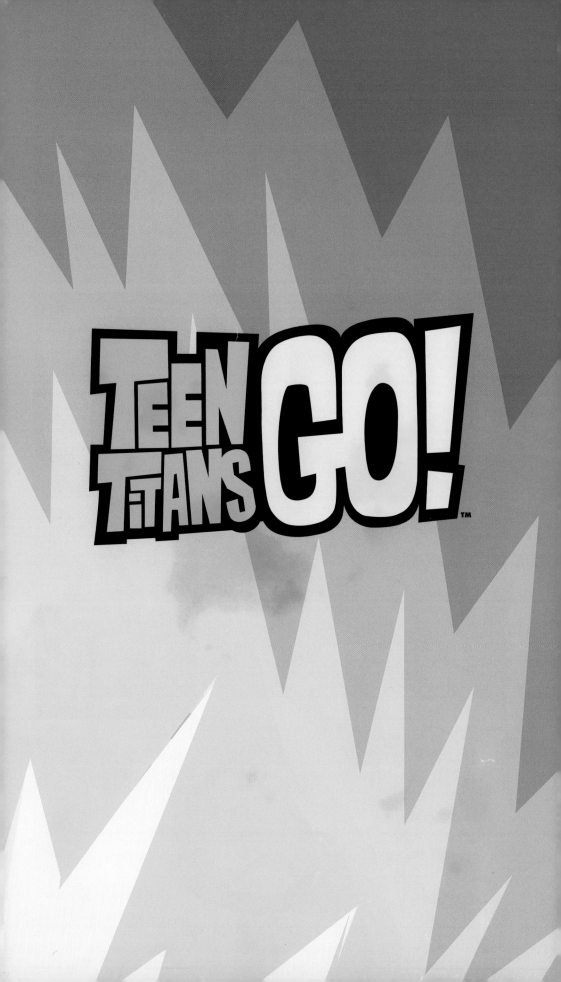